ALMOST SISTERS
THE SISTERS WAR

Other Books in
the ALMOST SISTERS Series
by Kathryn Makris
from Avon Books

THE SISTERS SCHEME

Coming Soon

THE SISTERS TEAM

KATHRYN MAKRIS is the author of a number of books for young adults, some of which have been translated into Spanish, Italian, French, and German. She also works as a reporter and has published articles in *Mother Jones* magazine, the San Francisco *Chronicle*, and other publications. Her interview credits include the Reverend Jesse Jackson, Ralph Nader, Gloria Steinem, Sissy Spacek, Ted Danson, "Colonel" Sanders, and Benji the dog. The ALMOST SISTERS trilogy are her first books for middle grade readers.

She enjoys hiking, swimming, nature study, and travel, migrating regularly between California and the state she grew up in, Texas.

ALMOST SISTERS
THE SISTERS WAR

KATHRYN MAKRIS

AN AVON CAMELOT BOOK

THE SISTERS WAR is an original publication of Avon Books. This work has never before appeared in book form.

AVON BOOKS
A division of
The Hearst Corporation
1350 Avenue of the Americas
New York, New York 10019

Copyright © 1991 by Kathryn Makris
Published by arrangement with the author
Library of Congress Catalog Card Number:91-92061
ISBN: 0-380-76055-X
RL: 4.9

First Avon Camelot Printing: November 1991

CAMELOT TRADEMARK REG. U.S. PAT. OFF. AND IN OTHER COUNTRIES, MARCA REGIS-TRADA, HECHO EN U.S.A.

Printed in the U.S.A.

OPM   10   9   8   7   6   5   4   3   2   1

This book is dedicated with innumerable thanks to Joanna Cole, whose enthusiasm and guidance led to *ALMOST SISTERS*.

Thanks to the Stepfamily Association of America in Lincoln, Nebraska, for helpful information and to Mary W. for that plus friendship.

Chapter One

"Pass the chips," said Ricki Romero, her dark eyes glued to her favorite television soap opera.

Her best friend and new stepsister, Vanessa Shepherd, handed her a jumbo yellow bag of nacho chips. Both girls dug into it, dipping their chips into the jar of salsa that sat between them.

"Don't spill sauce on the sofa," Vanessa warned. Like Ricki, she never took her eyes off the television screen. Wisps of blond hair had wandered out of her ponytail. Her toes wiggled inside her socks. She hugged her knees against her chest, making her small, slender body into a cozy ball under her cotton nightgown.

Ricki stretched her long legs to the coffee table, where her big, bare feet rested on a stack of old newspapers. One of her black pigtails snaked across the back of the sofa. The other dangled down alongside a dribble of sauce on her pajama top.

On the television screen, a man in baggy white overalls pointed a window-washing brush at a red-haired woman in ski clothes.

"I swear to you, Genevieve, it wasn't me!" he said.

"That man is Brett Burford," said Vanessa's Great Aunt Allegra. She sat in the old green armchair next to

1

the sofa, wearing a frayed, purple silk dressing gown, purple satin ballet slippers, and a purple turban over her dyed orange curls. "He escaped from prison in Brazil last week and now has returned to Miller City in disguise—see that fake mustache?—to find the true killer of his brother-in-law's ex-wife's father's business partner and prove that *he* didn't do it." Aunt Allegra took a satisfied sip of tea from her lilac-rimmed china cup.

Vanessa and Ricki nodded eagerly. Aunt Allegra had been filling them in on the background of "Day After Day" since Monday, when Ricki's mother and Vanessa's father had left on their honeymoon month in Maine. Now, three days later, they were hooked on the soap, along with "Mission: Impossible" reruns and "Oprah," Aunt Allegra's other favorite shows.

In fact, the girls got to watch TV all day, sometimes until the national anthem sign-off. Aunt Allegra let them stay up as late as they wanted. She let them do almost anything they wanted. The only thing she got fussy about was teeth. The girls had to brush three times a day, and floss, and gargle.

Otherwise, the week had been perfect. Exactly what Ricki and Vanessa had imagined when they first came up with the plan to become sisters almost a whole year before.

"Now that young woman trapped in the old mine shaft is Chelsea Smiley," said Aunt Allegra. "The man trying to rescue her is her grandfather, Wesley March, owner of the Triple Two Ranch, where Brett Burford's sister, Heavenly, had an argument with their brother-in-law, Nathan King, last winter, possibly leading to the

2

murder of Nathan's ex-wife's father's ruthless business partner, Corrinne.''

The girls watched breathlessly as the grandfather pulled with all his might on a rope to which his granddaughter clung. She was surrounded by squealing rats and flapping bats and rotting timbers. Then, suddenly, the whole scene started to shake and tremble.

"Heavens to Betsy!" clucked Aunt Allegra, blinking large blue eyes. "The mine shaft is collapsing!"

"Hold on, Chelsea!" called the grandfather. "Hold—"

He didn't get to finish, because a sudden jolt sent him sprawling headlong into the dust billowing from the mine shaft.

The next thing on the screen was a woman holding up a clean diaper beside a box of laundry detergent.

"Oh, my land." Aunt Allegra's wrinkly, pink face crumpled in a frown. "They're going to leave us hanging, aren't they?"

"Looks like it," agreed Ricki, munching up another chip.

"They're leaving Chelsea hanging, too," added Vanessa with a giggle. She knew her father would be horrified to see her watching a soap opera. Her dad believed that any TV program not on the educational channel was garbage.

He would also be horrified to hear that she hadn't touched her cello in three days. In six years of playing, she had never gone that long. This week, she was just having too much fun.

Ricki stretched her arms up over her head. She wondered what her mother would have to say about her wearing pajamas at two o'clock in the afternoon. Probably nothing positive. And nothing positive about the fact that Ricki and Vanessa hadn't actually changed out of their nightclothes in three days.

Ricki hadn't even gone outside to practice pitching softballs, as she was supposed to do before the start of the second summer season in July. She just hadn't gotten around to it.

Ricki's mother, Anita, and Vanessa's father, Andy, had both said that while they were gone, Aunt Allegra made the rules. And so far, Aunt Allegra's rules were great.

"I believe I'll go upstairs for my afternoon nap," Aunt Allegra said. From the coffee table she began gathering up the silver tea service and tray that she had brought with her in a gigantic suitcase all the way to California from Virginia last week, when she came to stay with them just before the wedding.

"Need some help, Aunt Allegra?" asked Ricki.

"No, dear, thank you," the old woman answered with a smile. "I'll just take these into the kitchen."

The girls watched her. Small and light, Aunt Allegra moved so fast that she always seemed on the brink of toppling over. But as she tottered off on her cane, she balanced the tea tray in her other hand like an expert waitress.

Vanessa leaned over and whispered to Ricki, "Didn't I tell you she'd be great?"

"Yup." Ricki stretched a brown-skinned leg up in the air. "She's the best."

"And isn't this exactly how we thought it would be, Ricki?" Vanessa sighed and nestled into the sofa cushions. "It's the best summer vacation I've ever had!"

"Me, too," Ricki said. "Like one long sleepover."

"An endless pajama party! And it's forever!" Vanes-

4

sa's green eyes turned to her friend. "We're really sisters now."

Ricki's ink black eyes sparkled back. "Just like we planned!"

"Hooray for the Sisters Scheme!" Vanessa cheered.

"Shh!" Ricki held a finger over her lips, giggling. "Aunt Allegra will hear you!"

Vanessa giggled, too. "Don't you think everyone already suspects?"

"That it was us who fired up a romance between your dad and my mom?" Ricki asked.

"*And* cooked up a scheme to get them married," Vanessa added.

Ricki tapped a finger on her chin. "I think your dad and my mom suspect, a little. But what could have been more natural? Your dad, divorced. My mom, a widow. You and me, best friends. Perfect match!"

"I'm so glad we thought of it. Goodness knows it hadn't occurred to *them*. I mean, on the outside, your mother and my father seem so different."

"I know. Your dad the rock 'n' roller," Ricki said.

"Your mom, the banker," said Vanessa.

"Hey, Mom's not a banker. She's an investments advisor. There's a difference."

"Well, for that matter, my father is not a rock 'n' roller. He's a composer and musician."

Ricki shrugged. "Anyway, they never would have gotten together if we hadn't planned those outings and stuff to make them get to know each other."

"That's for sure," agreed Vanessa. "And I don't think they started to catch on to the Sisters Scheme until toward the end."

Ricki folded her hands behind her head. "You know what, Vee?"

"Hmm?"

"I like being sisters. And I like living here. I'm glad your dad got this old place and fixed it up last year. I'm glad you and Mom and I helped on it, too, 'cause it makes it feel more like home."

"Oh, Ricki, I'm glad, too. Every summer vacation that I can remember I've been so lonely. Now I've got a sister!"

"And best friend, all in one!" Ricki pointed out.

"Let's see, we've been friends for three and a half years, since we were eight," Vanessa counted up, "and sisters for . . . five and a half days!"

"Way to go!" Ricki held her hand up for a high five. Vanessa slapped it merrily. "We did it!"

"Are you hungry?" Ricki asked.

"Famished." Vanessa nodded.

Ricki pulled out a box of fudge cookies from under the sofa and ripped it open. "Here. I was saving these for a special occasion. This is it! Let's celebrate!"

"Yes!" Vanessa popped a cookie into her mouth. "What do you want to watch next on TV?"

"Um, 'Beverly Hillbillies,' " said Ricki.

"Do we have to? That show is so dumb." Vanessa wrinkled her nose.

"No, it's not," Ricki said through a mouthful of cookie. "It's funny."

"Let's watch 'Wild Kingdom,' " Vanessa said.

"Are you kidding? *That's* dumb."

"It is not," Vanessa insisted.

"Is, too," Ricki said. "Besides, we watched it yesterday, so it's my turn to choose."

"Oh, all right." Vanessa finally gave in. "**But** tomorrow it'll be my turn."

"Deal." Ricki nodded and got up to change the channel. "Wish you had remote control. When Mom comes back and we pick up the rest of our stuff from the condo, we'll bring over our TV."

"Ricki!"

"What?"

"Your cookie crumbs!"

"Huh? Which cookie crumbs?"

"The ones you just spilled all over the rug when you stood up." Vanessa pointed downward. "They were in your lap."

Ricki sighed. "Vee, a few cookie crumbs never hurt anything." She flipped the TV tuner knob, then brushed a couple of crumbs off the rug into her palm. "There. Happy?"

Vanessa shrugged. "I guess."

That evening Aunt Allegra made sloppy joes and pineapple salad for dinner. The girls scooped strawberry ice cream into three huge bowls for dessert. They all did the dishes together and watched two movies in a row on TV.

By the time the national anthem came on, and Aunt Allegra put her hand over her heart as she did every time she heard it, Ricki and Vanessa felt so sleepy they could barely drag themselves upstairs to bed.

"Don't forget your teeth, dears," Aunt Allegra called.

Vanessa sighed. Aunt Allegra had once illustrated a set of children's books on dental hygiene.

"Okay, Aunt Allegra," Ricki answered, although the last thing she cared about at that moment was dental

7

hygiene. Her pillow looked a lot better than her toothbrush.

"Ricki," Vanessa mumbled groggily when they entered their bathroom. "You did it again."

"Did what?" Ricki blinked.

"The toothpaste. You left the cap off."

"So?"

"It leaked on the sink."

"Oh," Ricki mumbled back. She was too tired to say anything else. But while she squeezed toothpaste onto her brush and stuck it in her mouth she wondered how anyone could be as picky as Vanessa was about such dumb things: toothpaste, cookie crumbs.

Vanessa brushed sleepily, wondering how anyone could be as messy as Ricki.

Minutes later they tumbled into their twin beds on either side of the room.

"Good night," Vanessa muttered.

" 'Night," answered Ricki. She fell asleep almost right away.

Vanessa lay awake. The house was a mess. Her dad would have a fit if he saw the piles of newspapers in the living room and the crumbs on the rugs. Just thinking about running the vacuum made Vanessa feel much better. Finally she dozed off.

But no sooner had she fallen asleep than she heard Ricki calling to her.

"What?" Vanessa slowly stirred awake. "What is it?"

"*Ooo-aah-aah!*"

"Vee, what's wrong?" Ricki asked.

"What's wrong with *you*, Ricki? Why are you making such weird noises?"

8

"Me? I'm not making any noises. You woke me up."

"You woke *me* up," Vanessa countered.

"No, I didn't. I was asleep, and I heard this awful—"

"*Ooo-aah-aah!*"

Vanessa held her breath. "There it is again! Ricki," she whispered, "that was really you, wasn't it?"

Ricki's eyes widened. "No, Vee. Are you sure it wasn't you?"

"It wasn't me. Oh, my!" Vanessa gasped.

"What?" Ricki demanded.

"Well, if it wasn't me and it wasn't you—"

"It must have been Aunt Allegra," Ricki finished.

"But it didn't sound like Aunt Allegra. Not at all," Vanessa pointed out. She had started chewing on the inside of her cheek, which she always did when she felt nervous.

"I know, but it's got to be her," Ricki said firmly. "Turn on your light."

Vanessa shook her head. "I can't."

"Why not?" Ricki asked.

"I'm under the covers."

"Are you hiding?" Ricki bit her lip.

"Yes. Why don't you turn on *your* light?" Vanessa suggested.

"Because I'm under the covers, too," Ricki admitted.

Vanessa told herself to stay calm. "Ricki, we have to do something. What if—if Aunt Allegra has hurt herself. Or what if—"

"Let's not say what if, Vee. It's too scary. Listen, I've got an idea. We'll count to three, then we'll both get out of bed and turn on our lamps, okay?"

Vanessa took a deep breath. "Okay. Ready?"

9

"Ready."

"One . . ." the girls began. "Two . . . Three!"

They both jumped up as they'd promised, flipped on their lamps, and stared at each other as another loud moan echoed in the hall right outside their door.

Chapter Two

Vanessa and Ricki froze in terror. It sounded as if a very large, deep-voiced creature—definitely not Aunt Allegra—wanted to come in.

"Vee!" Ricki whispered frantically. "What should we do?"

"The lock!" Vanessa whispered back, finally able to think. For a minute it seemed her brain had stopped working.

Ricki flew at the door and turned the rusty old key until it made a loud, clanky click.

"Oh, no!" Vanessa gasped.

"What?"

"He must have heard that. Now he knows we're in here!"

"Who?" Ricki frowned.

"The—the burglar."

"You think it's a burglar? But why would a burglar moan?" Ricki bit at a thumbnail.

"What else could it be?" Vanessa's fair skin had paled to sheet white.

"If only you had a phone in here," Ricki said in a shaky voice, "we could call the police."

"Or a dog," Vanessa added.

"We could call a dog?" asked Ricki.

"No!" Vanessa rolled her eyes. "I meant, if we had a dog it would scare the burglar off."

"That's it! If the burglar tries to come in we'll start barking like big, bad dogs. Then I'll get my softball bat, and you'll get your cello, and we'll stand behind the door and—"

"But what about Aunt Allegra? What if—" Vanessa stopped, because she realized that the moaning had suddenly stopped. There was silence.

The girls stared at each other. Ricki bit her lower lip. Vanessa's lip trembled.

"We've got to go out there," Vanessa whispered, chin jutting out bravely. "To make sure Aunt Allegra is all—"

Once again she was interrupted, this time by a loud knock on the door.

Ricki squealed, grabbed Vanessa's hand, and dashed toward the window.

"Girls?" asked a voice from the hall.

Vanessa turned back to the door. "Ricki, that's Aunt Allegra!"

"May I come in, dears?"

Ricki was panting so hard she could barely breathe. Vanessa ran to the door and unlocked it.

In tottered Aunt Allegra on her cane. She kissed Vanessa on the forehead. "I saw your lights on and thought I'd come in for another pair of good-night kisses. Oh, my, Ricki dear. You're flushed. Is anything the matter?"

Ricki caught her breath. "Aunt Allegra, didn't you— Were you—Didn't you hear something?"

"Pardon, dear?" Aunt Allegra cupped a hand over her ear. "Did I what?"

"Ricki is just saying that she's fine," Vanessa interrupted loudly. "Have you turned down your hearing aid for the night, Aunt Allegra?"

"Oh, yes. I have, dear."

"Well, Ricki's fine. Aren't you, Ricki?"

"Fine? I'm fine?" Ricki tried to figure out the look Vanessa shot her. "Well, I guess . . ."

"Yes, she's fine, Aunt Allegra." Vanessa smiled. "We're sleepy, that's all. We were just going to bed."

"That's good, dears. Pleasant dreams." Aunt Allegra gave Ricki a kiss on the forehead.

Vanessa walked with the old woman into the hallway, waited until she was safe in the guest room, then ran back into her room with Ricki. "We're being silly," she said. "My father installed a burglar alarm, remember? No one could have gotten in quietly."

Ricki nodded. "Anyway, why would a burglar moan and groan?"

"Maybe it was the wind," Vanessa said. "Maybe the wind is blowing in a different direction than usual tonight, and since this is an old house . . ."

"Or it might have been Aunt Allegra coming up the stairs," Ricki suggested. "She has arthritis in her knees, right? That probably makes her moan and groan sometimes. Anyway, why wouldn't you let me ask her about it?"

"We shouldn't frighten her. She's eighty years old."

"You mean, we might scare her if we tell her about the noises and she says she didn't make them?" asked Ricki.

Vanessa chewed on her cheek. "It certainly didn't sound like Aunt Allegra, did it? Or like the wind."

"Vee, let's not talk about it anymore." Ricki yawned in exhaustion, but at the same time she got a cold shiver just thinking of how spooky those noises had been.

Vanessa yawned, too. "I'll lock the door."

"Yeah!" Ricki agreed, crawling into bed. "How about if we keep a light on?"

"Excellent idea." Vanessa left her lamp on and slipped under her covers.

Neither girl shut her eyes.

"Ricki?" Vanessa whispered.

"Yeah?"

"I'm glad you're here." Of all the sisters in the world, Vanessa thought, Ricki was probably one of the messiest, but she was also one of the very best.

Ricki smiled. "I'm glad you're here, Vee." Picky or not, Vanessa made a pretty good sister, especially when it came to scary nighttime noises.

Within seconds, they were both sound asleep.

"Good morning, dears," Aunt Allegra chirped the next day at breakfast.

She still wore her old purple dressing gown and ballet slippers. But today there was no turban over her crop of tight curls, which reminded the girls of lambswool. That is, on a lamb dyed a bright, brassy shade of carrot.

"Did you sleep well?" Aunt Allegra asked.

"Oh, fine, thanks," Vanessa said.

Ricki thought, *Sure, minus a few moans and groans around midnight*.

"How about you, Aunt Allegra?" asked Vanessa. "How are your knees?"

"My knees? Oh, same as usual, dear. I've grown used to the old creaky bothers. Can't let them stop me, you know. I walk everywhere in my little town back in Virginia."

"And your knees don't hurt a lot, Aunt Allegra?" asked Ricki. "For instance, when you're climbing stairs?"

The old woman leaned her head to one side in thought, looking for a moment very much like her great grandniece Vanessa. "Well, yes. I'd say they do quite a bit sometimes."

"Sometimes," Vanessa probed, "they might hurt so badly that you might cry out, or moan or something?"

"Oh, dear!" Aunt Allegra shook her head, laughing. "It's not that dreadful! But how sweet of you both to be concerned for me. Truly, I'm fine. I'm very happy to be staying here with the two of you. Such lovely girls. I've never felt better." She smiled, showing even, shiny white rows of teeth.

The girls smiled back. Vanessa was happy that her great aunt felt healthy. The problem was, if it wasn't Aunt Allegra moaning and groaning just outside their door last night, then who—or what—was it? Could it really have been just the wind?

"As I was saying about my little hometown, Sweeney," Aunt Allegra said, "you and your dear parents really must come visit me. Do you promise? I have so many friends who would enjoy meeting you."

Ricki tapped a finger on her chin. She found it hard to concentrate on what Aunt Allegra was saying. Instead, she thought about the wind, old houses, scary noises, and just how tired she and Vanessa had been the night before. Maybe they had let their imaginations run away with them.

"To newcomers," Aunt Allegra was saying, "Sweeney may appear to be a tiny, dull village, but you'd be surprised to discover how many fascinating inhabitants there really are. Hundreds of thousands."

"Really?" asked Vanessa. "But Sweeney is a small town, isn't it?"

Aunt Allegra smiled strangely. "Yes. But there are uncounted numbers of souls there. You see, it's such a pleasant hometown that no one ever wants to leave. Of course, people may have to leave physically, but their spirits always remain with us."

Vanessa nodded. "Oh, I see. That's a nice idea. Just like I had to leave my grandparents behind in Boston when my dad and I moved here to California five years ago, but I feel that in a way, I'm always with them. And my mother is a singer and has to travel all the time, but we write letters sometimes to sort of stay in touch."

"That's right, dear," Aunt Allegra said.

"I kind of feel that my dad is with me, too, sometimes," added Ricki. "I mean, he died when I was three, but I do remember him a little, and Mom says he'll never really leave our hearts."

"Yes, Ricki, my dear. What a lovely thought." Aunt Allegra's eyes got misty, and she pulled a lavender lace hanky from the pocket of her dressing gown. "My dear departed Marlon, your late great uncle, Vanessa, lives in my heart, too. Although he hasn't come back home yet."

"Come back home?" asked Ricki, frowning. "But I thought he—I thought your husband was—"

16

"Marlon passed away four years ago, dear. But you see, my neighbor, Flora Carlson, has three of them in her house, and it hardly seems fair."

Vanessa tilted her head to the side. "Three of what, Aunt Allegra?"

"Three spirits: Edgar, Lucille, and Captain Le Beau." Aunt Allegra blew her nose.

Ricki's dark eyebrows knit together. "Spirits? You mean people who died, who she keeps in her heart?"

"In her *house*, dear." Aunt Allegra dabbed at her eyes. "And they don't happen to be Flora's relatives, although they have become rather dear friends to her."

"In her *house?*" asked Vanessa in a small voice.

"Flora has a lovely home. It's no wonder she'd attract so many of them. Edgar actually lived in it at one time. He came to Sweeney as a lumber man in the 1870s. Poor Captain Le Beau's ship foundered right off our coast in 1902. And Lucille—"

"Aunt Allegra," Vanessa interrupted. "Are you saying that these . . . people . . . are . . ."

"Spirits, my dear. Spirits."

"You mean *ghosts?*" Ricki's eyes got huge.

Aunt Allegra laughed. "Well, I suppose that is one term. But it's not the one they prefer."

"They?" Vanessa asked. "The . . . spirits?"

Aunt Allegra nodded.

"They talk to you?" Ricki blinked in amazement.

"Oh, no, not to me. As I said, none have come to share my home. Although I can't understand why not. Most older houses will have a spirit or two, unless someone has taken pains to drive them off, and I certainly haven't. Never would."

Vanessa sucked in a breath. "How old does a house have to be to have . . . spirits in it, Aunt Allegra?"

"I couldn't say, Vanessa. But I imagine a soul would want to feel settled and secure, in a good, solid building. Not in one of those newfangled, modern places that go up overnight."

Vanessa started gathering the breakfast dishes. "So, for instance, *this* house . . . it's old, isn't it?"

"Oh, yes, I would think it's quite old enough. Very pleasant, as well. I'm sure a spirit or two would feel at home here."

Ricki gulped. A spirit or two? Aunt Allegra had to be joking.

Vanessa took another deep breath. Aunt Allegra couldn't be serious.

Ricki got up and piled her dirty dishes in the sink.

While puzzling over Aunt Allegra's story, Vanessa frowned at the dishes. The pile was so high it looked ready to fall over. Why couldn't Ricki use common sense once in a while? She picked up half the dishes and moved them to the countertop.

Ricki carried the plastic milk jug to the refrigerator. Vanessa followed her and snapped on the jug's little plastic top, which Ricki had left off.

"Oh, we've forgotten to collect the mail this morning, haven't we?" said Aunt Allegra. "I'll be right back."

As soon as she left the room, Vanessa whispered, "You don't believe any of that, do you, Ricki?"

"Which part?" asked Ricki, trying to sound casual. The whole thing was so spooky that if she let herself get serious, she'd also get scared.

"*All* of it," Vanessa said. "I've never believed in ghosts or anything, but, what if—"

"I hate it when you say 'what if,' Vee. It gives me the creeps."

"But do you think it's possible? Last night, what if that noise . . ."

Ricki put her hands over her ears. "I don't want to talk about that noise. I thought we agreed it was the wind."

"I know we did." Vanessa chewed on her cheek. "That's the only logical explanation. I really don't believe in ghosts."

"Me, neither," said Ricki.

Vanessa sighed. "Then let's stop talking about it."

"That's what *I* said."

"All right." Vanessa nodded. "Anyway, it's already ten o'clock. What do you want to watch on TV?"

" 'Hollywood Squares!' " Ricki tossed the dish towel into the sink and made for the living room. "I've got dibs!"

Vanessa picked up the dish towel and hung it neatly above the sink, then chased after Ricki. "Yuck! I hate 'Hollywood Squares.' "

They raced to the TV to see who could turn it on first.

At eight o'clock that night, they were still watching television.

"Oh, look, girls! Oh channel six there's a movie called *Madness of the Dark,* to celebrate the fact that today is Friday the thirteenth." Aunt Allegra read from the TV listings in the newspaper, " 'A retired college professor discovers mysterious beings in an old castle and must invent a chemical potion to destroy them.' Doesn't that sound chilling?'' She giggled.

Ricki wasn't sure she felt in the mood for mysterious beings. Neither did Vanessa. They both had had enough excitement for one Friday the thirteenth. But after ten minutes of *Madness of the Dark*, they were perched on the edge of their seats.

"Maybe this is a bit too . . . stimulating for us,'' Aunt Allegra said, gazing at them worriedly over the rim of her teacup. "We could watch something else.''

"Oh, no!'' Vanessa cried.

"Really, we're fine,'' said Ricki, who was biting her thumbnails.

The mysterious beings were supposed to be ghosts of people who in life had been pretty rotten. They looked like large actors in gorilla suits with cooked spaghetti glued all over their heads. Finally they took over the castle, the town, and were on their way to the next when the retired professor sprayed them with sticky blue goo from a crop duster airplane.

"Such nonsense,'' Aunt Allegra clucked as the words "The End'' rolled up on the screen.

"Nonsense?'' Vanessa repeated. "But I thought you believed in ghosts and things.''

"Spirits, dear,'' corrected Aunt Allegra. "Yes, but I've never once heard of one attempting a bit of harm. Except in the movies, of course.'' She laughed.

"So you're saying Edward and Lucy are harmless?'' Ricki asked.

"Edgar and Lucille,'' said Aunt Allegra. "And let's not forget the Captain. He wouldn't want to be ignored.''

20

"Edgar and Lucille and the Captain. They're not . . . scary?" asked Ricki.

"Of course not." Aunt Allegra sipped her tea. "Well, perhaps a bit at first, before one gets to know them, but then they're very much like you or me, with the same feelings and moods, ups and downs. It may be a bit unnerving at first to hear a spirit sobbing in a corner or pacing back and forth along a hallway. . . ."

"Or moaning and groaning?" asked Vanessa.

"Certainly. Yes, I believe Mr. Hauptman the grocer has a spirit who moans. It's his great-great-grandfather Lyman, a cranky old curmudgeon, I'm sorry to say."

Vanessa and Ricki traded looks.

Could it be that they had a cranky, moaning and groaning ghost of their very own?

Chapter Three

On Monday morning, Ricki tossed her softball toward the ceiling and caught it just before it hit the coffee table.

She sat on the living room sofa, tossing the ball again and again.

In the armchair, Aunt Allegra worked the newspaper crossword puzzle. Vanessa was upstairs. They had all gotten tired of TV, and there was not much else to do. Ricki felt so bored that in the morning she had even gotten dressed for a change of pace.

What was taking Vanessa so long? She'd gone upstairs to get dressed, too, but that had been half an hour ago. Maybe, if Vanessa ever came down, she'd help Ricki practice her softball pitch in the backyard.

The ball was about three feet above the lamp next to the sofa when Ricki heard a moose grunting. For a second she froze, wondering what could be making the deep, sad noises. Then she saw her softball ding the lamp shade, bounce off the end table, and head for Aunt Allegra.

She caught it just in time.

"Did you hear that, Aunt Allegra?"

"Hear what, dear? Your ball?"

"No. That . . . other noise."

Aunt Allegra looked up from her crossword puzzle and listened. "Perhaps I did hear something, faintly. It seemed to—"

She was interrupted by the low, mournful moan again. But this time it was worse, sounding even more deep and sad.

"Oh, my gosh!" Ricki leapt to her feet. "Aunt Allegra, it's coming from upstairs!"

"Yes, I do hear it now, dear. But I think it may be—"

Ricki didn't hear the rest of what the old woman said. She was so scared that all she could think of was how awful the moaning sounded—like a large, sick animal. Then she realized that Vee was upstairs in their bedroom—all alone!

Though her knees wobbled, Ricki took the stairs two at a time. She ran through the hall, and just as she reached the door to the room it happened again.

"Aay-eee-ooh!"

This time it was *inside* the bedroom!

"Vee!" Ricki cried, bursting open the door.

She found Vanessa sitting in her desk chair, bow poised over the strings of her cello. "What's wrong, Ricki?"

"Where is it?" Ricki panted.

"Where is what?" Vanessa frowned, annoyed about having her first practice all week interrupted.

"The—the spirit!"

"Spirit? Ricki, what—"

"Didn't you hear it, Vee? It was in here!"

"You heard the spirit?" Vanessa raised her eyebrows.

"Yes! This really sickening sound, like—"

23

"Ricki, I've been sitting right here looking at my music—Wait a minute." Suddenly Vanessa smiled. "Go back into the hall."

"Huh? Why should I do that?"

"You'll see."

Ricki frowned but went out.

"Now shut the door behind you," Vanessa said.

"Okay, but I'm telling you I—"

"Oh, Ricki, just do it, all right?"

Ricki slammed the door shut. In seconds she heard a low, sad wail coming from inside the room, followed by a deep thumping. She grabbed the doorknob but stopped just before turning it.

Something about the noise sounded familiar this time. Very familiar. In fact, Ricki was positive she had heard it even before that day.

She finally stepped back into the room wearing a big grin. "I bet you think this is funny, Vee."

Vanessa pulled her bow across the lowest part of the cello's strings, making another deep sound. "I bet you do, too."

"Now that I'm not petrified anymore, I guess it is funny."

Vanessa giggled and plucked the strings softly to make the deep thumping sound.

"Okay, okay, I get the message." Ricki laughed. "But it couldn't have been you making those noises the other night, because you were right in here with me."

"Correct." Vanessa rested her bow in her lap. "You know, I really think the noises were made by this house somehow. It's an old house, and sound seems to carry in strange ways, doesn't it?"

Ricki nodded. "You can say that again. From downstairs, that cello of yours sounded like a wounded buffalo!''

"Thanks a lot!" Vanessa huffed. "I happen to be practicing a very difficult part of a sonata."

"Written for the cello or for a sick cow?" Ricki asked.

Vanessa stuck her tongue out at her. "You try playing it sometime. We'll see how you do."

"No, thanks. One lost baby hippo per household is plenty." Ricki giggled.

"Lost baby hippo!" Vanessa raised an eyebrow.

"Hello?" came a voice from the doorway.

"Oh, Aunt Allegra! Vanessa's fine. I forgot to tell you. She was just—"

"I know." Aunt Allegra smiled. "Practicing her cello, wasn't she?"

Vanessa nodded. "Ricki says I sound like a lost baby hippo."

"Well, that does happen. I played the fiddle, myself, in my youth. My sister Lottie, Vanessa's grandmother, stuffed her ears with cotton whenever I practiced."

The girls laughed.

All afternoon they giggled over stories Aunt Allegra told them. They sat on the deck off the kitchen, enjoying the June breezes and almost a gallon of cherries they picked off twin trees in the backyard.

"Can you believe," Ricki asked that night as she squeezed toothpaste onto her brush, "what Aunt Allegra said about that grocer guy?"

"That he tried to drive his great-great-grandfather's spirit away by burning old newspapers dated Friday the thirteenth?" Vanessa raised an eyebrow. "What I can't believe is that he and Aunt Allegra and the rest of their

25

friends in Sweeney actually think these spirits exist. Especially Aunt Allegra. She's so sensible.''

"That's the weird part," Ricki agreed. "I mean, your great-aunt is not some kook, but she truly believes in ghosts. Nice ghosts, maybe, but a ghost is a ghost, right?"

Vanessa nodded. "She's *your* great-aunt, too."

"Huh?"

"Now that we're sisters, you can't say she's just *my* great-aunt."

"Oh, that's right." Ricki grinned. "Share and share alike."

"Ricki," Vanessa said, tearing a length of dental floss from the little canister in the medicine cabinet. "I'm starting to feel spooked again about all this ghost business. Those stories about the grocer's great-great-grandfather and everything kind of scare me, even though—"

"I know. Me, too. I don't believe them, either, but it's like watching scary movies on TV. They're so fake there's no way you can believe them, but you can't help getting the creeps anyway."

"Ricki!" Vanessa whispered.

Ricki glanced over to see her friend's cheeks go as pink as Aunt Allegra's. "What is it, Vee?"

"Your towel!" Vanessa stared at the yellow washcloth that Ricki had just dropped onto the sink's countertop.

Ricki stared at it, too, and froze in the middle of dragging a brush through her tangled black hair. "What? Is—is there a spider or something?"

Vanessa shook her head. "No. Why didn't you hang it up?"

"Huh?" Ricki scrunched up her nose.

"You didn't hang your towel up."

Ricki shrugged. "So what?"

Vanessa let out an exasperated sigh. "This place is a pigpen."

Ricki rolled her eyes. "One little washcloth never hurt anything."

"It's not just one little washcloth, Ricki. It's all your washcloths. All your towels. All your clothes. You never hang them up. You leave dirty pajamas and underwear and socks all over the floor in our room. And after meals I have to remind you to put your dishes in the dishwasher."

"Nobody said you *have* to remind me," Ricki argued. "You just like to. You like to nag me."

"Oh, I'm sure." Vanessa crossed her arms. "I get my thrills out of nagging you. All day long I just wait for my chance."

"Yeah, I think you do. You've been bugging me ever since I moved in here, Vee. You've turned into the Clean Police."

"Well, *you've* turned into a slob! I refuse to live like this. It's disgusting."

"You're nuts." Ricki narrowed her eyes. "Everything's got to be just so or else you blow your top."

"*Just so?* I'd settle for being able to walk to my bed without tripping over your softball mitt!"

"Then maybe I should just go home." Ricki lobbed her hairbrush into her suitcase, which lay on the floor in the middle of the room.

"What do you mean, 'go home'? This *is* home."

"No, it's not. Most of my stuff and Mom's is still

at our condo. I'll just go back there to live." Flopping down on her bed, Ricki started braiding her hair.

"Ricki, you know your mother is going to stop renting the condo. You're going to move all your stuff over here as soon as my father and your mother get back."

Ricki bit her lower lip. She felt awful. Homesick, even, for the first time that month. She really liked living with Vanessa. Vee was absolutely her best friend in the whole world, even though she fussed about stupid things. But it was hard to feel at home with Vanessa bugging her all the time. She felt as if she couldn't make a move without Vanessa finding something wrong with it. Those scary noises the other night hadn't helped, either. And to top it all off, tomorrow was her birthday! If only her mother were there!

For a minute, she thought about calling her mom. Anita and Andy had both told the girls to call if anything urgent came up. Did being miserable count as urgent? Probably not. Ricki sighed.

Vanessa hated to see Ricki sulk. It made her feel guilty about being such a nag. Especially since tomorrow was Ricki's twelfth birthday. But it was awfully hard not to nag someone as messy as Ricki. As long as Ricki was messy in her own house, back at the condo, Vanessa didn't mind. In fact, it was kind of fascinating to watch people as messy as Ricki and Anita in action. Vanessa had been impressed by the height of dirty dish stacks in their kitchen and the mountains of unfolded laundry in their living room. But in her own house, especially her own room, it made her feel nervous and on edge to have things out of order.

If only her dad were there. Barely a week of the honeymoon had passed. Already that was longer than

Vanessa could remember having been apart from her father. As soon as he came back, she knew he would help her get things straight again and show Ricki how nice it was to have an organized household.

Vanessa sighed. "I'm sorry, Ricki. I don't mean to pester you. It's almost your birthday, too."

Ricki shrugged and sighed again. "I guess it's okay, Vee. You're used to things a certain way. Want me to get my stuff off the floor?"

"Oh, not now." Vanessa shook her head. "We're sleepy. Let's go to bed."

Ricki yawned.

As they headed for their beds, they heard footsteps in the hall.

"Oh, good," Vanessa said. "Aunt Allegra is coming to say good night. I wanted to ask her what time we're going to your Uncle Mario's deli for your birthday party tomorrow."

"He's *your* Uncle Mario, too, now, remember?" Ricki climbed into bed.

Vanessa laughed. "Oh, absolutely! How could I forget? It's great to have an uncle with a Mexican food deli!"

"I'm getting cabin fever around here," said Ricki. "We haven't been out since Mom and Andy left."

"I wish Aunt Allegra could drive." Vanessa laid her head on the pillow and sighed.

"Aunt Laura said she'd take us to the movies next week," Ricki pointed out. Her mother's sister had promised not to let them get too bored while Anita and Andy were away on their honeymoon.

"Meanwhile, we're going grocery shopping with Gordon and Suzanne on the weekend," Vanessa said.

Her father's old friend and band partner, Gordon Taylor, and his sweet girlfriend, Suzanne Marchand, were always fun.

The footsteps stopped right outside the door.

"Come in, Aunt Allegra," Vanessa called.

There was no answer.

"Aunt Allegra?" Ricki shouted.

"Hmm," said Vanessa. "That's funny. I could have sworn . . ."

"Me, too." Ricki frowned. "I definitely heard footsteps. Aunt Allegra, are you out there?"

"Maybe she can't hear us," Vanessa said. "She removes her hearing aid at night."

"Oh. Then why doesn't she knock, or say something?"

Vanessa shrugged. "Maybe we should find out."

"You mean open the door?" Ricki pulled the covers up to her nose.

"Are you scared? I am," confessed Vanessa.

"It's probably just the wind again, right?" Ricki asked.

"Yes, it must be. I think you're right."

"All the same, we should look and see," said Ricki.

"I suppose we should, shouldn't we?"

Ricki and Vanessa threw back their covers and crept slowly toward the door. Together, they put their hands on the doorknob and turned it. Opening the door just a tiny crack, the girls peeked into the hall.

It was dark. And almost dead quiet. Only the sound of a light breeze stirring the leaves outside drifted in from the small window at the hall's far end.

"Should we go down to Aunt Allegra's room?" asked Ricki. "See if she wanted anything?"

"Well . . ." Vanessa chewed on her cheek. "I suppose."

They tiptoed down the hall side by side. Vanessa couldn't imagine why she felt so scared. It was silly. The house was perfectly safe. Dad had made sure of that with the burglar alarm and lots of locks before he left.

Ricki felt embarrassed to have such shaky knees. There's no such thing as ghosts, she told herself over and over. No such thing.

She and Vanessa had just reached the door to the bathroom when they both heard a tremendous *thunk*.

They froze.

Vanessa turned to look at Ricki but couldn't see a thing. It was so dark!

In the next instant, though, it didn't matter to her whether it was dark or not. She and Ricki were running absolutely as fast as they could to get away from the clattering of footsteps right behind them!

Chapter Four

Ricki didn't bother to knock on Aunt Allegra's door. She reached it just seconds before Vanessa and flung it open.

Vanessa barreled in right behind her, slammed the door shut, and leaned against it.

For a while they panted and trembled so hard they didn't notice Aunt Allegra smiling at them from her bed.

"Well, hello, girls." She wore her reading half-glasses and a purple nightgown. A book sat propped up in her lap.

"Oh, Aunt Allegra," Vanessa managed to say between gasps for air. "We're so sorry to barge in on you, but . . ."

"Didn't you hear that?" Ricki blurted, still leaning against the door for support.

"Hear what, dear?"

"Well, they're gone now, but there were footsteps," Vanessa explained, "right out there in the hall!"

"Footsteps?" Aunt Allegra took off her glasses. "In the hall? Oh, my. You don't suspect a prowler, do you?"

Ricki shook her head. "This is so spooky. We think it might be a—a—"

Swallowing, Vanessa gathered her courage. "A ghost. I mean, spirit. We're afraid we have one in the house."

Aunt Allegra smiled, folded her glasses, and laid them neatly on her bedside table. Then she shut her book and laid it there, too.

"A spirit, my dears? Hmm. A spirit," she said, "is nothing to be afraid of. Now let's go have a look."

"Yuck," said Ricki, pulling a mangled green blob out of a box in the laundry room. "What do you think this is?"

"Let me see." Vanessa frowned. She wasn't completely comfortable with the idea of going through all seven packing boxes. Her dad had piled them up in the laundry room so he could take them to a thrift shop when he got back. Filled with stray junk from all over the house that earlier residents had left behind, the boxes smelled dank and musty.

But Vanessa knew she and Ricki had a mission. Over mugs of steaming milk and honey the night before, Aunt Allegra had explained exactly what they needed to do.

First, a thorough search of the house had turned up no burglars or loose-hinged windows to account for the noises. Next, to find out if the noises had been caused by a ghost, the girls would have to do some research, Aunt Allegra said.

"This blob," said Vanessa, peering at the green thing, "may at one time have been a plastic plant, although it has now lost most of the resemblance. I don't think a ghost would be attracted to a house by a deformed plastic plant, do you? Aunt Allegra said we have to look for evidence that someone has had powerful feelings about this house."

33

"*You* had powerful feelings about this house," Ricki pointed out. "You hated it."

"I did not."

"You did, too. When your dad first bought it and said you guys were going to leave Mrs. Quan's duplex to live here on Mariposa Lane, you were miserable."

"That's because this house was such a wreck. It looked like it was going to fall apart. Broken windows, sagging stairs, wrecked plumbing . . ."

Ricki nodded. "But I knew it would turn out great, with just a little elbow grease."

"A little? It took six months just to fix it so we could move in!"

"Let's see, if I really loved the house, and you really hated it . . ." Ricki tapped a finger on her chin. "Which of us will come back here as a ghost?"

"Oh, Ricki, stop. That's creepy."

"Well, doesn't it make you feel creepy going through all this old stuff? I mean, who knows how old some of it is or who it belonged to."

Vanessa nodded. "It's sort of like going through people's lives."

"You know, this is dumb, Vee. I don't believe in ghosts. Why are we doing this?"

"You believed in them last night."

"Yeah. Ghosts make sense in the middle of the night." Ricki bunched her mouth to the side.

"Well, I don't believe in them, either." Vanessa dropped an old shirt back into the box.

"You really don't?" asked Ricki.

"I really don't."

"Then let's just forget about it, okay?" Ricki rubbed her arms to chase off a shiver.

"Let's." Vanessa took the plastic plant from Ricki and put it in the box.

"That plant thing looks like a dog chewed it," said Ricki.

Vanessa sighed. "I wish *we* had a dog. It could tell us if we had a ghost. Dogs can sense that sort of thing."

"When my mom and your dad come back you're supposed to get one, right?"

"I can hardly wait." Vanessa's eyes shone happily. But at the same time, she felt a sort of pang inside, the same one she felt whenever she thought about her father and how much she missed him.

Ricki saw the weird look on her friend's face and felt sorry for her. Vanessa wanted a dog so badly she seemed about to cry over it. Ricki felt a little sniffly herself. But that was because she had let herself think about how much she missed her mom.

"Let's go outside and pitch balls," she said.

Vanessa wrinkled her nose. "I don't want to pitch balls."

"Then what do you want to do?" Ricki sighed.

"How about a game? Parcheesi or something."

"We need more people," said Ricki.

"Aunt Allegra will play with us," suggested Vanessa.

"But it's no fun with only three. I wish we knew some kids around here."

Vanessa nodded. All their friends from school were either busy or out of town. Louise Ann was helping at her mother's African imports boutique all summer. Kimberly was staying with her father on a ranch in North Dakota. Dani and her parents had gone back to the Philippines for a family reunion. Ricki's old condo complex was too far away to have the Steinberg kids visit. And the Murdoch twins, Marlys and Mavis, from Vanessa's old neighborhood, had been sent by their mother to a fly fishing camp, even though they both hated seafood.

"I wish we could walk around and look for some kids."

"But Ricki, Dad said—"

Ricki rolled her eyes. "I know what he said. Mom said it, too. We can't leave the house by ourselves until they come back."

With a third sigh, she helped Vanessa close the box and stack it with the others along the wall. Then the girls wandered into the living room to wait for "Day After Day" to start.

Both girls felt much better that afternoon. First, Anita and Andy called long-distance to wish Ricki happy birthday. Later, Uncle Mario, Ricki's mother's tall, stout, and jovial brother, took them and Aunt Allegra to his deli.

His wife, short, round Aunt Ruth, made a big fuss over Ricki's birthday. She and Uncle Mario cooked Ricki's favorite Mexican dish, enchiladas with a special peanut sauce, and a huge caramel ice-cream cake. Afterward, Ricki opened her presents, then she and Vanessa played soccer with Ricki's little cousins Anthony and Carlos in the patio area behind the deli.

When Uncle Mario dropped the girls and Aunt Allegra off at home that evening, they were all tired and happy.

The next day, Vanessa spent most of the afternoon with her cello. The familiar touch of the strings under her fingers and the weight of her wooden bow in her other hand gave her a calm, comfortable feeling.

Playing a piece she'd memorized years ago, an old French lullaby, she thought of her mother. The sound of the cello often reminded Vanessa of her, because Mama's voice was smooth and clear, just like the instrument's.

Drawing her bow across the strings, Vanessa sighed. She had to admit, she really missed her mother. It had been over a year since they'd seen each other. And there was no telling when Mama might visit next. As far as Vanessa knew, her mother was singing at a hotel in Hawaii. But she hadn't heard from her since the telegram that almost interrupted Andy and Anita's wedding. It arrived just as Anita started to walk down the aisle. Vanessa had never been so worried. After weeks of near disasters before the wedding, she thought that it might be the last straw to ruin everything.

But the telegram said only that Mama was in Hawaii, sent her best wishes for the wedding day, and would visit soon.

Soon. What did that mean? With Mama, you never knew.

Maybe one of these days she would write with an address. Or maybe Mama had written to her own mother, Nona, Vanessa's grandmother. Vanessa decided to ask Nona about it during their weekly phone call on Sunday.

Meanwhile, she had better concentrate on her music. Suzanne and Gordon would be coming to drive her to her cello lesson tomorrow, and she was supposed to have two new pieces memorized.

Downstairs, Ricki stayed busy taking pictures of Aunt Allegra.

"Can you, um, kind of turn a little?" she asked her model.

"Turn?" Aunt Allegra frowned. "Which way?"

"Your chin. Angle it a little to the left, the way you do when you're thinking about something."

"Oh, do I?" Aunt Allegra blushed.

"Perfect!" Ricki snapped several shots of the pose.

Ricki was in heaven. For her birthday Uncle Mario and Aunt Ruth gave her ten rolls of black and white film, to go with the fancy camera they had given her last year. With ten rolls, she could play and experiment, instead of having to make every shot count, the way she did when her mom was bugging her about spending too much money on photography.

By the end of the summer, Ricki wanted to have a new set of best shots to show to the photography teacher at the junior high.

Her stomach got the jitters at the idea of starting junior high. At the same time, the idea was exciting. Roosevelt Junior High was supposed to have a real photography lab and real photography classes. Plus, she and Vanessa and their friends from Kennedy Intermediate—Dani and Kimberly and Louise Ann and the others—wouldn't be just kids anymore. They'd be junior high students!

The camera stopped clicking. Ricki checked the frame meter and saw the number thirty-six. End of the roll. Darn. The rest of the film was upstairs in her and Vanessa's room, where Vanessa was practicing cello.

It was bad enough having to listen to the moaning moose sounds from downstairs, but now Ricki would have to be in the same room with them while looking for the rolls of film.

"I'll be back, Aunt Allegra. I've got to get more film, okay? Don't move."

Aunt Allegra lifted an eyebrow, just as her grandniece often did. "I can't move?"

"Hey, that's a perfect pose, right there. Yeah, don't move an inch, okay?"

Ricki ran up the stairs and down the hall. Whistling, she marched into the room toward her half of the closet.

Vanessa stopped in the middle of a piece, because it went so fast she couldn't take her eyes off the music sheet without fumbling. She cleared her throat. What, exactly, did Ricki think she was doing?

Now where could that camera bag be? Ricki wondered. Still whistling, she knelt on the floor of the closet tossing shoes, dirty socks, and two softballs out into the room behind her.

Vanessa cleared her throat again. "Ahem!"

Finally, Ricki found her old canvas shoulder bag in the very back of her side of the closet. She sat cross-legged on the floor, rummaging through it for a roll of film, then looked up to find Vanessa staring at her.

"Hi, Vee. You through practicing?"

Vanessa kept staring. "No. I am not."

"Oh." Ricki found a stick of grape bubble gum in the camera bag. She unwrapped it, popped it into her mouth, wadded the wrapping up, and tossed it into the closet.

"I stopped practicing," said Vanessa, "because I was interrupted."

Ricki kept searching through the bag. "By what?"

39

"Do you have to make so much noise when you come in?"

"I just wanted to get my stuff." Ricki blew a large bubble and popped it.

"Can't you do it quietly?"

"Pop my gum?"

"No! Barge in here!"

"Well," said Ricki between bubbles. "You don't practice quietly. It drives me crazy."

Vanessa placed her bow in her lap, gearing up for a fight. "*I* drive *you* crazy?"

"Yeah, you do. Anyway, I didn't know it would bug you if I came in here."

"It wouldn't bug me if you tried to be quiet. But how can it not bug me when you have no consideration? It would bug anyone."

"Not me. You're too picky. Everything bugs you. You're easily bugged. Maybe it's because you're still a kid."

"Still a kid?" Vanessa repeated. "What do you mean by that?"

"I mean, you're eleven. I'm twelve."

"So? I'll be twelve in August."

"That's two months." Ricki popped another bubble.

Vanessa's green eyes blazed. "It doesn't give you a right to be inconsiderate."

"I'm not inconsiderate."

"You are, too."

"Am not," Ricki snapped. "*You're* inconsiderate, because you make me feel like everything I do is wrong."

Vanessa sighed in exasperation. "All right, look. *You* sit in this chair and try to concentrate on . . . on multi-

40

plication tables or something while I barge in here like you did.''

"I know my multiplication tables, Vee.''

"Hah, but I bet you can't concentrate on them while I make as much noise as you did!''

"Can, too,'' Ricki countered.

"Cannot,'' Vanessa shot back.

Ricki rolled her eyes but took Vanessa's place in the chair.

Vanessa left the room. She burst back in whistling.

"One times one equals one,'' Ricki began. "One times two equals two.''

Vanessa stomped to the closet.

"One times three equals three.''

A white sneaker came flying out of the closet.

"One times four equals four.''

Next came a paper shopping bag full of old schoolwork.

"One times five equals . . . one times five equals . . .'' Ricki couldn't go on.

Vanessa glared at her from the closet. "See, you can't concentrate, can you?''

"It's not,'' Ricki managed to say between giggles, "that I can't . . . concentrate. Its just that . . .'' She had to stop to giggle again.

"What's so funny?''

Ricki pointed at Vanessa. "You! You!''

With a hand on her hip, Vanessa kept glaring.

But Ricki was almost doubled over with laughter. "I mean . . . you're squatting down there, throwing stuff around, making a big mess. You never throw stuff around. You never make messes. This is great!''

"I dare you to get up to six times six,'' Vanessa said, eyebrow raised.

In between giggles, Ricki tried to go on. "One times five equals five, one times six . . ."

Vanessa couldn't help it. She laughed, too. She supposed she did look pretty funny tossing things out of the closet. And Ricki looked awfully funny, too, trying to gasp out "equals six" in between laughs.

Gazing at the mess in the room and at the now bare closet floor, Vanessa laughed along with Ricki. After a second or two, though, she frowned. On her side of the closet floor, at the very back, she noticed a short, narrow gap in the boards.

On her hands and knees, Vanessa crawled into the closet. Her hanging clothes brushed the top of her head as she went.

"Hey, aren't you going to toss more stuff?" asked Ricki.

Vanessa stared into the gap in the floorboards.

"Vee, what are you doing in there?" Ricki walked toward the closet, collecting sneakers and gum wrappers as she went.

Just then, Vanessa crawled out. In her hands, she held a small black chest. She kneeled with it in her lap and blew a thick layer of dust off the top.

The dust flew up at Ricki. She coughed. "Uff! What the heck—uff!—is that?"

Silently, Vanessa loosened a tiny brass hook from its slot on the chest's shiny black lid. As she lifted the lid, the pungent scent of cedar drifted out.

Inside, a stack of yellowed paper envelopes lay tied together with pale pink satin ribbon.

"Holy kazoo!" whispered Ricki.

Chapter Five

Vanessa squinted at the postage stamp on the first envelope, a tiny picture of a boat in a harbor. It was clearly marked with the date 1936.

"I can't believe this!" she whispered.

The address was in pale blue ink, done in tall, spidery handwriting.

" 'Miss Clementine Hewitt,' " Ricki read aloud. " '202 Mariposa Lane, Berkeley, California, United States of America.' "

Vanessa's eyebrows shot upward. "202 Mariposa Lane! That's here! That's our house!"

"Wow!" Ricki said, breathlessly. "How cool. Who's it from?"

Vanessa flipped the envelope over. "It doesn't say. There's no return address."

"Well, then look inside." Ricki took the envelope from Vanessa and pulled out a folded, narrow sheet of yellowed paper. It was crowded top to bottom with the same spidery handwriting that was on the envelope.

"Oh, look!" cried Vanessa. "At the bottom it says, 'Our ship won't be in port again until next month. I'll write again soon with return post information. Until then, dear Clemmie, I am and ever shall be . . . Your devoted admirer, Emmett Tibbs.' "

43

"Hey, it's a love letter!" Ricki grinned. "Wow, look at the beginning!"

The girls read silently:

Dear Clementine,
Far and wide I may wander as a sailor aboard this trading vessel, but never shall I forget my afternoons in the lovely Hewitt parlor, nor your kind mama's gracious Sunday dinners. I think only of the end of this voyage next year, when I shall return to feast both my eyes and my bowels in your lovely home.

"His bowels?" Vanessa repeated. "Bowels? Those are *guts*. Disgusting! That doesn't sound very romantic!"

"I know," Ricki agreed. "The guy sounds like a freeloader to me. He just wanted to come back for more Sunday dinners."

Vanessa raised one eyebrow, thinking. "He sure did seem to like this house, didn't he?"

"Yeah, let's read the next letter."

Vanessa clutched the stack to her chest, away from Ricki. "No."

"Huh?" Ricki frowned. "Why not?"

"Because they're not ours. They're Clementine's."

Ricki rolled her eyes. "Vee, Clementine left them in our closet."

"It must have been her closet at the time. And she went to a lot of trouble to hide them. They were in a secret compartment."

"A secret compartment? Really? Where?" Ricki ducked her head into Vanessa's side of the closet to look.

Vanessa pointed at the little gap in the floorboards.

"Wow! This is so cool! But you know, if Clementine cared so much about these letters, why didn't she take them with her when she left?"

"Who knows?" Vanessa shrugged. "But I really don't think it's right to read someone else's letters."

Ricki rolled her eyes again.

"Besides," Vanessa added, "if we read them without permission, it might upset Emmett."

"Emmett? How would he ever know?" Ricki cocked her head. Then she narrowed her eyes at Vanessa. "Wait a minute, Vee. You're not thinking what I think you're thinking, are you?"

Vanessa leaned back against the closet doorjamb. "Well, it makes sense, doesn't it? Aunt Allegra says spirits are attracted to houses for certain reasons. Emmett really liked his Sunday dinners here. And maybe he was in love with Clementine, too."

"This is wild!" Ricki shook her head. "Almost better than 'Day After Day.' "

"Don't you think it fits?" Vanessa asked.

"I have to admit, it kind of does."

"Oh, Ricki, isn't this exciting? Now we know about our spirit!"

"We only *suspect* about our spirit, Vee." Lying on her side, Ricki stretched out and rested her head on a palm. "We won't know for sure until we read the letters, will we?" She grinned.

Vanessa pursed her lips. "Out of the question. We have to ask Clementine first."

"Ask Clementine! How?"

Vanessa carefully bundled the letters together and shut them back into the little cedar box. "I don't know.

Let's go talk to Aunt Allegra. I bet she knows all about this sort of thing."

"Aunt Allegra!" Ricki cried. "Heck! I forgot all about her! I told her not to move!"

But Aunt Allegra had moved. The girls found her in the kitchen making tea. At the table, she put on her glasses and shook her head in amazement while reading the first letter. "This is quite a find, girls. Just what we were looking for. Bravo!"

"Really, Aunt Allegra?" Vanessa said, beaming. "Do you really think we have a spirit here? That it might be Emmett?"

"It is possible, dear. Entirely possible."

"How about reading the letters?" Ricki asked. "Wouldn't that be helpful?"

Aunt Allegra took off her glasses and tapped them against her shoulder. "Well, Vanessa found these letters, and her feeling seems to be that we mustn't read them. Perhaps we should make an effort to find this young woman. . . ."

"Clementine Hewitt," Vanessa said.

Ricki sighed. "She's no young woman anymore. These letters are from the 1930s, and this is the 1990s."

"Well, we can only try. Shall we look in the telephone directory?" Aunt Allegra suggested.

There were exactly forty-three Hewitts listed in the Berkeley area telephone book, and over the next three days, in between an outing with Gordon and Suzanne and a movie with Aunt Laura, Vanessa and Ricki managed to reach all but seven of them.

It was frustrating. Some numbers they had to call over and over before anyone answered. Others were busy all the time or had answering machines. And sometimes, the Hewitts they reached weren't very nice. One man yelled that he was up to his ears with callers trying to find long-lost Hewitts.

On the morning of the Fourth of July, Vanessa awoke feeling a little glum. Maybe they'd never find Clementine Hewitt or anyone who knew her. In the meantime, not reading the letters was awfully hard. Sometimes her fingers actually itched with the urge to take them out of the box in the closet. Of course, she'd never admit that to Ricki, who was already pestering her to no end about how harmless it would be to read a few letters.

The exciting thing about the day, though, was that it was July fourth, which meant there was only one day left before July fifth, when her father and Anita were coming home!

Trudging downstairs a half hour later, Ricki heard the high-pitched whine of a bottle rocket firing off somewhere in the neighborhood. She sighed. On every Fourth of July she could remember, her mother had taken her out to the city fireworks displays. This year she'd have to settle for just hearing them, since Anita and Andy wouldn't be home until tomorrow. But the very thought of her mother coming home cheered her up. Just one more day!

All afternoon the girls sat on the backyard deck off the kitchen with Aunt Allegra. It was too hot to stay inside. Vanessa thought she would melt. Some of the pages of her library book, *Treasure Island*, had stuck together. Ricki lay sprawled out on the hammock, swinging back and forth, leaning over once in a while to play jacks on the picnic table. Aunt Allegra dozed in a chaise lounge.

"Don't you ever get tired of reading?" Ricki asked, frowning at Vanessa.

"No," Vanessa answered. A fly buzzed by her nose, and she swatted at it.

Ricki sighed. "But you read *constantly*."

Vanessa ignored her.

Ricki rolled out of the hammock. "Let's play badminton."

"It's too hot."

"Oh, don't be a wimp."

"I don't feel like it, Ricki."

"All right, fine. Be a deck potato." Ricki stalked off into the kitchen.

Vanessa sighed and turned another sticky page.

As Ricki rummaged in the cupboard for a snack, she heard the sound of an engine in the driveway. Too late to be the mail truck. Probably just one of those salespeople. She peeked through the dining room curtains.

Aunt Ruth's van!

"Hey," she called out to the deck. "Aunt Ruth and the kids are here!"

Followed by Vanessa and Aunt Allegra, Ricki dashed to the front door. Opening it, she found Aunt Ruth carrying a suitcase and little Carlos and Anthony struggling up the front path with one flight bag each.

Vanessa gasped. "Wait! That suitcase is—"

Just then the girls saw two more people carrying two more suitcases.

Ricki was the first to take off running. "Mom!" she yelled at the top of her lungs.

Vanessa was right behind her, heading straight into her father's arms.

*   *   *

48

"Did we really surprise you?" Anita asked after giving Ricki the twentieth or so hug in a row. Her dark eyes sparkled.

Along with Vanessa, Andy, and the kids, they sat on a picnic blanket in the park under a golden sunset, waiting for the Fourth of July fireworks. Aunt Allegra and Aunt Ruth had lawn chairs set up next to them.

Following the flurry of hugs and hellos at home, Andy and Anita had insisted that everyone pile back into the van for dinner out and the fireworks show.

"You sure did surprise us!" Vanessa nodded.

Ricki wagged a finger at her mother and Andy. "We thought you weren't coming home till tomorrow."

"That's what we thought, too," Andy said, giving her and Vanessa one of his big grins. "But we both got homesick."

"We really missed the two of you." Anita's long, slender arms pulled Ricki and Vanessa to her sides for more hugs.

Vanessa beamed at her father. She had never seen him look so happy, except maybe at his and Anita's wedding the month before. He had let his brown beard grow longer than usual, and he actually had a tan for the first time Vanessa could remember.

"America the Beautiful" began to play on a loudspeaker, and everyone joined in singing. Ricki noticed that her mother's face looked smooth and calm, free of the worry lines that usually tightened it. Anita's high cheekbones glowed cinnamon brown, framed by her short black curls.

At the very instant that the last note of "America" played, the sky burst into a sparkling shower of red, white, and blue with the first of the fireworks.

"Heavens to Betsy!" cried Aunt Allegra merrily.

The little cousins let out whoops of joy.

Standing between tall Anita and shorter Andy, Ricki and Vanessa held tightly to their parents' hands and gave each other quick, smug grins. Thanks to the Sisters Scheme, they were together at last. A family!

"Oh, now, Vanessa. No tears!" Aunt Allegra gave her a little pat on the shoulder. "And don't look so glum, Ricki."

"We can't help it," Ricki said. "We're sad that you're going."

People milled around them in the airport waiting area, rushing to catch planes or to pick up luggage.

Aunt Allegra wore a purple felt hat with a long orange feather and a pretty purple dress. She carried her silver-tipped black cane, all ready to go. Only she, Vanessa thought, could wear such a crazy outfit and still look good. Vanessa tried to smile. She had known all along that her great-aunt was scheduled to leave the day after Dad and Anita got home, but she couldn't help sniffling. She hated good-byes.

Ricki took hold of the old woman's hand. "Mom and Andy promised we can visit you in Sweeney next summer." Ricki had no relatives as old or as interesting as Aunt Allegra. Things wouldn't be the same at home without her.

Anita nodded and smiled. "That's right, it's a promise."

"Good." Aunt Allegra squeezed Ricki's hand. "Meanwhile, girls, will you write to me? Keep me up to date on Emmett and Clementine?"

Vanessa nodded. "Dad says he'll help us find her."

50

Out of the corner of Ricki's eye, she saw her mother raise an eyebrow at Andy. He gave a little shrug back.

"A spirit in the house is a true blessing," said Aunt Allegra. "Your home is destined to be a very happy one."

Andy grinned. "Well, you've gotten us off to a good start, Aunt Allegra, by taking such good care of the girls for us."

"We can't thank you enough," Anita added, giving Aunt Allegra a hug. "We only wish you could stay longer."

"Thank you, dear. It was every bit my pleasure. But I must hurry home for our annual Huckleberry Festival next week. Well, off I go, my girls." She swept Vanessa and Ricki into her arms for one last hug. Then she positioned her cane and pegged with it down the ramp to the airplane gate. "Good-bye, dears! Remember your teeth!"

The girls and their parents stood and waved. Anita gave Vanessa fresh tissues to blow her nose. Ricki kept sighing sadly. Then Anita needed a tissue for herself, and by the time the plane took off, Andy had misty eyes, too.

It wasn't until they were in Anita's small car on the way home that Andy cheered up and said, "Hmm. Emmett and Clementine, huh?"

Anita shook her head. "You girls aren't taken in by all the ghost talk, are you?"

Vanessa and Ricki looked at each other.

"What do you mean, 'taken in'?" Vanessa asked.

"Well," Anita said as she drove onto the bridge crossing San Francisco Bay, "I mean that ghosts don't exist."

51

"Except around the campfire," added Andy, "or late at night when you're bored."

"Wait a minute," Ricki said. "Last night at dinner, when Aunt Allegra was explaining to you about spirits, you didn't say anything."

"We thought you believed us," said Vanessa.

"Oh, honey, how can we believe that there's a . . . a spirit in our house?" Anita chuckled.

"But we heard it!" Ricki countered. "On two different nights!"

"I'm sure you heard something." Andy turned around in the front seat to look back at the girls. "But you didn't hear a ghost."

Vanessa pursed her lips. "Dad, Aunt Allegra really thinks it is a ghost. And she should know, because—"

"Because her friend Flora has three of them." Andy nodded. "Yeah, I heard. Vee, Aunt Allegra is a wonderful woman. Always my favorite aunt. She's very intelligent, too. The problem is that she's got some set ideas that may be fine for Sweeney, but they just don't fit elsewhere."

Ricki wasn't sure what to think anymore. In her head, believing in ghosts was hard to do. But every time she remembered that eerie moaning right outside the bedroom door and the loud footsteps that chased her and Vanessa down the hall, she got a cold shiver.

"Does this mean you won't help us look for Clementine?" she asked Andy.

"Sure I will," he answered. "I believe *she* exists, or at least she did at one time. Although finding her may not be easy. Oh, Anita, watch out up ahead. Don't miss the turn for the Nimitz freeway."

"I'm not taking the Nimitz," Anita said. "I'm staying on Highway 92."

"You are? But you'll end up taking Highway 13," said Andy.

"Right." Anita took off her sunglasses. "Which is much faster."

Andy shook his head. "It's out of the way."

"Andy, look at the map if you don't believe me." Anita pushed the button to open the glove box.

"Wait. I'll do this, Anita. You just concentrate on driving."

"I am concentrating on driving. I always do. If you didn't try to tell me wrong ways to turn—"

"It's not the wrong way," Andy objected.

"It is." Anita put her sunglasses back on.

"It's not," insisted Andy, then busied himself with the huge map.

Anita sighed loudly.

Ricki forgot all about the creepy feeling of hearing ghosts. Instead, she got another creepy feeling, the same one she had gotten in the weeks just before her mother married Andy, when it seemed the two of them were fighting about every little thing and might not ever get married.

Vanessa chewed on her cheek, wishing her father and Anita would go back to lecturing her and Ricki about ghosts. That was a lot better than listening to them argue.

She looked at Ricki. Ricki looked back at her. Then Anita pulled to a stop on the side of the highway to frown at a spot on the map that Andy had circled.

Neither Ricki nor Vanessa said a word to each other. They knew what they had to do.

"But I'm telling you," Andy was saying, "we'll end up in Timbuktu if you—"

"Excuse me," Ricki interrupted. "I've gotta go to the bathroom." She tried to sound urgent.

"Now?" her mother asked. "We were just at the airport, honey. Why didn't you—"

"I do, too," echoed Vanessa. "I have to go."

Her father looked at her.

She shrugged. "It was probably the apple juice we had at lunch."

"Right," agreed Ricki. "I really have to go now."

Anita sighed, then pulled into the freeway's exit lane.

Ricki gave Vanessa a tiny wink. It had worked! No more arguing! Andy stopped giving Anita directions. Anita stopped complaining about it. The two of them were now united in a common family goal—to find a gas station.

Chapter Six

The rest of the weekend went much more smoothly. In fact, Vanessa decided that Sunday was one of the nicest days in her whole life.

After a breakfast of waffles, she and Ricki, Andy and Anita sat out on the back deck reading the paper and laughing about Anita's attempts to teach Andy to water-ski on the lake in Maine. Then Vanessa and her father cleaned the house together while Ricki and her mother went to their condo to pick up some clothes and things. In the evening they all went to see a funny movie at a drive-in.

But Monday morning Vanessa awoke to the sound of an elephant charging down the stairs.

Ricki bolted upright in her bed. "*What* was that?"

"It means Dad *has* to believe us now!" Vanessa cried and flew out the door.

Ricki followed her to the top of the stairs.

There stood Anita with wet hair, in her bathrobe, trying to pull on a pair of panty hose.

"Did I wake you, girls? Sorry. This is my first day back at work, so I decided to go in early, and I was dressing out here so as not to wake Andy, but then I bumped into that darn laundry basket and sent it tum-

bling down the stairs. Some cat burglar I'd make!"
She'd gotten one leg into a stocking and was working
on the other one. "Now that you're awake I'm going
to use your bathroom to do my hair, okay?"

"We'll never get back to sleep," Ricki grumbled as
they watched her mother rush into the hall bathroom,
trailing the electric cord of her hair dryer.

Vanessa shrugged. "It's almost seven. I like getting
up early. Come on, we can watch the sunrise from our
room."

"Sunrise?" Ricki yawned. "No way. If I'm gonna
be awake, I've gotta eat."

In the kitchen, the girls heated up cinnamon bagels.
After a few minutes Anita hurried in wearing a slim-
fitting gray suit and black high heels. She was followed
by Andy in his pajamas.

He rubbed his eyes sleepily. "Well, hi, folks. This
is the crack of dawn crew, huh?"

"Sorry." Anita chuckled, putting the coffeepot on
the stove. "I was *trying* to be quiet."

He came up behind her and kissed her ear. "Next
time try to be noisy, and see what happens."

He joined Ricki and Vanessa at the table for a bagel,
while Anita kept bustling about the kitchen.

"Here, Mom," Ricki said, holding the plate out.
"Want one?"

She shook her head. "I've got to run if I'm going to
catch that seven-thirty train. All I need is my cup of
coffee."

"Here, let me help you," Andy offered, getting up.

"Oh, no, no." Anita waved him back down. "How
complicated is making a cup of coffee?"

As Vanessa watched Anita trot back and forth from

the stove to the cupboard to the sink to the stove and back again, she decided that making a cup of coffee must be very complicated. Just watching Anita was making her dizzy. And nervous. Anita acted so anxious about getting to work early that it was making Vanessa feel anxious, too. Because her father worked at home, he never had to rush around in the mornings.

"Did you forget your coffee maker at the condo, Mom?" Ricki asked between drinks of milk.

Anita nodded. "I'm afraid so. I left it right inside the door as we were leaving yesterday."

"You've got to eat something, Annie," Andy said, using his new pet name for his wife. "How about if I wrap up a bagel for you?"

Anita gave him a quick smile. "Okay." She planted pecks on the tops of Vanessa's and Ricki's heads on her way out the door. "See you tonight, sweeties."

Andy followed her into the hall, wrapping the bagel in waxed paper as he went.

Vanessa sighed in relief. It was as if a tornado had just left the room.

But then Anita charged back into the kitchen. "Almost forgot my car keys!"

"You're driving?" asked Andy.

"I've got to get to the train somehow," Anita answered.

"How about the bus?" Andy suggested.

"The bus? The bus stop is all the way at the end of the street. I'd have to walk there."

"Public transportation saves gas, it's better for the environment, and the walk would be good for you," said Andy.

Anita grabbed her keys off the countertop. "I don't have time for this discussion now."

"That's because you get up too late," Andy said.

"Look who's talking!" Anita turned on her heel and headed out through the hall.

Ricki bit at a thumbnail. Her mom and Andy had been back from their honeymoon for only two days, and already they were having a fight! She looked at Vanessa, who was worriedly chewing on her cheek.

Andy followed Anita out. "Annie," he said.

Vanessa listened carefully. If her father was using his nickname for Anita, he couldn't be too mad, could he?

"I'm sorry," he went on. "You're right. I shouldn't be hassling you about the environment this morning."

The girls heard Anita's soft laugh. "It's all right. I'm sorry, too. I shouldn't have lost my temper."

There were a few seconds of silence. Vanessa knew what that meant. She looked at Ricki and winked. Ricki winked back. Their parents were kissing and making up.

After a while the girls heard Anita's car roar off to the train station, then Andy's sleepy footsteps headed back into the house.

Shuffling into the kitchen, he yawned again. "Anyone for omelets?"

"Yeah! I'm still starving." Ricki rubbed her belly.

She and Vanessa offered to help, but Andy just handed them the paper and told them to report on the news. While Vanessa read to him about the latest political campaigns and lottery winners, Ricki looked through the comics. She felt deliciously lazy. It was like being in a restaurant, with someone cooking for you. At home

with her mother, they had never cooked real break-
fasts—especially not on weekdays.

About midway through the omelets, the doorbell
rang.

"I'll get it!" Vanessa offered, and came back a
minute later with Gordon.

"Well, good morning!" Andy grinned at his tall
friend. "Sit down and have some eggs. What brings
you here so early?"

"Oh, I was going to drop off a few notes about that
new song in your mailbox," Gordon said, sliding his
khaki cap off his short black hair. "But I saw the lights
on and decided to go ahead and ring the bell." His dark
skin lit up with the grin he gave Ricki. "Good morning,
Ricki. How's life with these two Shepherds?"

"Okay," Ricki mumbled back. She didn't do much
more than mumble, because she was too busy trying to
hide. That is, to fit as much of herself as possible under
the table. It was embarrassing to have Gordon see her
in her pajamas. He was a good friend of the family and
all, but still, she wished Vanessa had given her some
warning before marching in with him.

All day Andy had a steady stream of visitors. After
Gordon, there were other members of their band, Fast
Forward. Then came the artist friends who Ricki recognized because of the messes they used to make working
on their projects in Andy and Vanessa's apartment.

It looked like today, at least, Andy wasn't going to
have much time to help the girls look for Clementine
Hewitt.

"Let's look for her ourselves," Vanessa suggested in
the middle of "Day After Day" that afternoon, when

59

Chelsea Smiley and Brett Burford were kissing so much that Ricki got bored.

"How?" Ricki shrugged. "We've run out of ways. Your dad said he'd call his friend who sold him this house and see if he knows anything about the old owners."

"Well, there must be other ways we can look on our own, at least for people who might have known Clementine. Maybe friends, neighbors . . ."

"Hey, yeah!" Ricki perked up. "Neighbors! Let's ask around and see if anyone around here remembers the Hewitt family."

"We're not supposed to go out alone," Vanessa reminded her.

"That was while our parents were gone. Let's ask your dad if we can go for a walk."

Vanessa shrugged. "It's worth a try."

To the girls' delight, Andy gave them the okay, warning them to stay on Mariposa Lane and to be back in an hour.

Ricki felt like a bird freed from the cage as she and Vanessa set off down the street. There was a big, bright sun overhead in a clear sky. "This is great! Maybe we'll meet some kids."

"I doubt it." Vanessa shook her head. "I've never seen any, except for those little preschoolers down on Lomita Avenue."

"Maybe the ones our age watch TV all day like we were doing. Maybe *they* think there aren't any kids around, too."

"I suppose. But you know, this really doesn't look like a neighborhood for kids, does it?" Vanessa asked.

60

Ricki nodded. "I was thinking the same thing. No sidewalks."

"Not only that," said Vanessa, "but the houses are so far apart, and kind of old-looking. Sort of . . . gloomy."

"Maybe that's because of all the big trees," Ricki suggested. "They make some of the houses and yards look dark. Ours doesn't because your dad painted it lemon yellow, and he and Mom planted all the flowers out front."

Vanessa retied the green ribbon on her ponytail as they passed their next-door neighbor's house. It had a gray stone front covered by a thick growth of ivy. "Our street is spooky."

"Yeah, what a great neighborhood for haunted houses!"

"Oh, Ricki, don't say that!" Vanessa frowned.

"Well, our house is haunted, isn't it?"

"I don't know." Vanessa tossed her ponytail back over her shoulder. "Sometimes I believe in Emmett, and sometimes I don't. I mean, we haven't heard him in a while."

Ricki sighed. "It's frustrating. Just when we start believing in him, he disappears. Well, are we going to try to find Clementine, or not?"

"Let's start with that house across the street," said Vanessa. "It looks smaller and sunnier than the others."

The girls walked up a short path bordered by orange marigolds and pushed the doorbell next to the orange door. After three more rings, no one had answered.

"I think these people work during the day," said Vanessa. "They're a young couple."

"You know," Ricki said, "I think we should try one of our next-door neighbors. Those houses look much older, so maybe the people there would have known about the Hewitts."

"Well, okay, but not the ivy-covered one. It's too spooky."

Ricki nodded. "Looks just like the castle in the movie about the spaghetti heads and the retired professor."

"Oh, my gosh, you're right! Eeuu!" Vanessa put a hand over her mouth as she and Ricki stared across the street at the ivy house. Then they giggled and ran in the opposite direction toward the white, Spanish-style house on the other side of their own.

But there was no one home there, either.

Vanessa looked at her watch. "We've already used up twenty minutes of our hour. Where should we go next?"

"Oh, let's just goof around." Ricki picked up a pebble and tossed it. "I'm sick of looking for Clementine. I wish you'd just let us read the letters."

Vanessa pursed her lips. "Wish all you want. Why don't we walk down to the end of the street?"

Ricki shrugged. "Okay."

There were no kids to be found anywhere on Mariposa Lane. The girls passed house after house with absolutely no signs of life inside, much less any kids playing.

As they neared the corner, Vanessa started fanning herself with the hem of her green blouse. "It is so hot." Her pant legs clung to her knees, damp with sweat.

"No, it's not. It's just summer, that's all. Nice and warm. You should have worn shorts." Ricki pointed at her own baggy, red cutoffs and loose blue T-shirt, a hand-me-down from her mom. "And why don't your roll up your sleeves?"

"Because I burn, Ricki, that's why. Some of us aren't lucky enough to have natural tans."

Ricki rolled her eyes. "So wear sunscreen. You're always complaining about the heat, but you—"

Midsentence, Ricki was interrupted by a loud squawk coming from the tree branches overhead. She and Vanessa squinted upward.

"That sounded like a duck," Vanessa said.

"Yeah," Ricki agreed. "It did. Can you see it?"

"No." Vanessa shook her head. "The leaves are too thick. It's like a forest on this corner. Ricki, look!"

Ricki's eyes followed Vanessa's pointing finger down into the little canyon below the road.

"There's a house in the forest," Vanessa whispered.

Ricki nodded. "Wow, I never noticed it before."

"Neither have I," said Vanessa.

Through a thicket of trees standing like long-haired guards, the girls could see the window of a brown wooden house. Suddenly, in the window, a face appeared.

Vanessa gasped. Ricki's eyes widened.

The person staring back at them—*frowning* at them, in fact—had spiky, wild-looking white hair and small, unfriendly eyes.

"Ricki," Vanessa whispered. "Let's go."

"We're not doing anything wrong," said Ricki, still gazing back at the person in the window. "They can't chase us off just for looking."

Vanessa tugged at her arm. "I don't care. Come on. This is spooky."

Ricki wouldn't budge. "Isn't that weird, just to look out the window and frown at people? What a friendly neighborhood, huh?"

Vanessa tugged again. "I *know* it's weird, Ricki. Come on!"

Ricki still wouldn't move. Even after she felt something cold touch her palm, she kept staring back at the face in the window. The second time she felt the cold thing on her palm, she rolled her eyes in exasperation and wheeled on Vanessa.

"Vee, what are you—" she began, then froze. Right behind her, edging ever closer, stood a huge, black, shaggy animal.

Chapter Seven

Vanessa took firm hold of Ricki's arm. "Don't move."

"But, Vee," said Ricki in a high, tight voice. "There's a—"

"I know. I scc him."

"It's a—a wolf!" Ricki gulped. "It's huge! And it looks hungry!"

To Ricki's surprise, Vanessa just smilcd. "Ricki, he is not a wolf. He's a big dog. Now be still a minute. Let's make sure he's friendly."

"Let's not." Ricki started to back away. She was not crazy about dogs, especially not big ones. In kindergarten a golden retriever had knocked her down and stolen her lunch sack.

This dog was the size of a small pony. His head stood almost as high as Ricki's chest. His fur was so thick and dusty that he looked more like an old rug than a dog.

"Oh, Ricki, look! He's wagging his tail." Vanessa cooed, "Hello, little puppy!"

Ricki shook her head. "He can wag it all he wants, but—"

The dog suddenly lunged at Ricki's hand and stuck out an enormous pink tongue.

Ricki jumped away. "Yuck!"

Vanessa laughed, and the dog cocked his head from side to side. Then he wagged his long tail so hard that his whole, big black body started wiggling with it. Finally, he seemed to give up trying to figure the girls out and rolled over on his back, stretching four plate-size paws in the air.

"Oh, you are adorable!" Vanessa squealed.

Ricki grabbed her by the shoulders. "Don't you dare pet it," she warned. "It could have rabies."

Vanessa sighed. "But he's so cute!"

"Cute?" Ricki repeated. "A kitten might be cute. Even a poodle might be cute. But that—*that* thing is not cute. Let's go, Vee, before it stands up again."

"Oh, Ricki, don't be silly."

Ricki was already pulling her down the street toward home. Vanessa glanced over her shoulder to find the dog still lying paws up, scratching his back on a crack in the pavement. He thumped his tail when he caught Vanessa looking back at him.

Vanessa loved animals, especially dogs. At home, all she had were her goldfish, Hugo and Hannah. Last summer when Andy bought the house, he told her one good thing about moving there was that they could have a dog, which they couldn't have had in their rented apartment.

As Ricki dragged Vanessa down the street, she could tell that if she let go, Vanessa would run right back to that animal and pet it. Probably even hug it. Or try to take it home! She knew how badly her friend wanted a dog. Someday soon, Ricki knew, she would have to face the fact of living with one. Someday, sure. But not now. And not *that* dog!

"Ricki," Vanessa said quietly, still glancing over her shoulder.

"What?"

"Look." Vanessa's smile was as big as Texas. "He's following us."

Ricki sighed. "Oh, great. Just great. Shoo, dog, shoo!"

The dog stopped, pricked his ears up, and cocked his head.

"Don't shoo him. He's sweet. Let's take him back to his house. He probably lives on the corner."

"You mean that house in the woods? The one that five minutes ago you couldn't wait to get away from?"

Vanessa had already marched down the street and caught up with the dog. He let his ears drop happily as he nosed Vanessa's palm.

"No, sweetie, I don't have anything for you to eat," she told him. "Sorry. Let's go home, now. Come on, fella!" She clapped her hands and walked toward the corner.

"Great. Just great," Ricki muttered, following Vanessa and the dog from the safe distance of several feet.

Vanessa waited for Ricki at the corner, looking a little doubtful herself. "There's no path down to the house."

Ricki shrugged. "Maybe if we just stand here and yell, that person will come to the window again."

Vanessa frowned. "What if they call the police on us or something?"

67

"Oh, so you *are* scared." Ricki grinned.

"Well, it does look spooky down there."

Ricki took a deep breath. "Let's just get it over with."

"Where are you going?" Vanessa asked. The dog stood beside her, pricking his ears up as Ricki took a step down into the woods.

"Where does it look like I'm going? Down to the house. Come on." She motioned for Vanessa to follow.

"Through the woods?" Vanessa asked, parting a veil of branches to fall in behind Ricki.

"Got any better ideas?"

The dog gamboled past the girls to lead the way. His tail stood high in the air, swiveling back and forth like radar. He kept his nose to the ground.

"He acts like he's never been here before," Vanessa said as she pushed another branch away from her face.

"*Now* he tells us," said Ricki. "Now that we're almost there."

They stopped at the edge of the woods. It opened to a clearing that might have looked something like a front yard if it hadn't been strewn with old, rotting logs, piles of dead leaves, and things that looked like different-sized cages covered with blankets.

"This is weird," Ricki whispered. "What could be in those cages?"

"Hush, Ricki." Vanessa chewed her cheek. "You're trying to scare me."

"I'm scaring *you?* This was your idea!"

Vanessa nodded. "All right, well, there's the front door. Let's—let's get it over with, like you said."

"Hey, where'd the mutt go?"

"The dog?" Vanessa glanced around them. "I don't know! He was here just a minute ago!"

Ricki suddenly shrieked. "Aieee!"

Vanessa felt a furry nudge against her leg. She looked down to find the dog between her and Ricki, nosing Ricki's palm.

"Yuck! I wish it would stop doing that!" Ricki rubbed her wet palm on her shorts. "Yuck!"

"He likes you." Vanessa scratched his curly head, then coaxed him across the clearing toward the small, rickety-looking front door of the house. "Come on, puppy. Come on."

The cement patio around the door was an obstacle course of broken clay pots, bicycle parts, and two glass fish tanks half-filled with murky water, but no fish.

When the girls finally crossed it, they stood face-to-face with a lion's head, in the form of a big brass door knocker. A brass plate underneath it bore the engraved initials C.H.

The dog squeezed between Ricki and Vanessa again. He positioned himself just in front of them, then sat down politely, looking up at the girls as if to let them know he was ready.

"Well, go ahead," Ricki said to Vanessa.

"Me? Why don't you do it?"

"Because you're the one who wanted to bring the mutt back. You knock."

Vanessa took a breath and lifted the knocker's big ring handle, which was made to fit right in the lion's mouth.

The dog wagged his tail in interest when she dropped

the ring with a loud clank back into the mouth. Then she did it again, wondering if it would be that wild-haired, frowning person who answered.

But no one came. The dog stopped wagging his tail and looked at the girls again.

"Why does he keep doing that?" Ricki eyed him uncomfortably.

"What, looking at us? I think he thinks this is a game. Or maybe he knows about doors and knocking and people answering."

"Well, no one's answering this one," Ricki pointed out.

"I'll try again," Vanessa said.

After four more knocks, no one had appeared.

The dog shifted on his front paws and sighed. He scratched his neck with a hind paw.

"That person we saw," Ricki whispered, "they must still be in the house. But they just don't want to come out."

Vanessa nodded, stroking the dog's broad back. "You're right about this neighborhood. It *is* a good place for haunted houses. I'm glad he's with us."

Ricki rolled her eyes. "*He's* the reason we're standing in front of this spooky house, waiting for a spooky person to answer the door."

"Ricki, is your heart beating fast?" Vanessa asked.

"Pounding."

"Mine, too. Are your palms sweating?"

"I can't tell. They've still got dog slobber on them." Ricki made a face.

"I was just thinking," Vanessa whispered. "That person. C.H. or whoever. He or she could be anywhere.

I mean, maybe they aren't even in the house anymore, but . . . outside somewhere.''

Ricki glanced around the patio area, fighting a tremendous urge to bite her thumbnails. "Like, out *here* somewhere?"

Vanessa nodded slowly, looking over her shoulder at the mysterious blanketed cages in the yard. "I—I think maybe we should—"

Ricki didn't wait for her to finish. And Vanessa didn't wait for an answer. Within ten seconds they had hurdled over the broken pots and bike wheels and fish tanks, and in another five they were charging up the wooded hillside. The dog crashed through the brush right behind them.

Vanessa never felt so happy to feel the broiling glare of sunlight as she did when they reached the street.

"Oh, my gosh!" she said, panting.

The dog bounded in circles all around her and Ricki, excited by the chase.

As soon as the girls caught their breaths, they started down the street toward home, with the dog at their heels.

"He's following us again," Vanessa said, still panting.

Ricki bunched her mouth to the side. "He's got to belong to somebody around here."

"Not necessarily," Vanessa said. "He could be a stray."

"Well, you're not going to help him get home by making him follow you."

"I'm not making him follow me," Vanessa protested.

"You keep looking back and smiling at him, and he wags his tail."

"I can't help it if he's friendly."

When the girls reached their own yard, the dog trotted out ahead of them onto the grass. After a couple of sniffs, he took off like a colt in a spring meadow, kicking up his heels, darting about, and snorting in delight. Then he lifted his leg over a tree root.

"Oh, Ricki, he likes it here!" Vanessa clapped her hands gleefully.

"Vee, he just—he just did *that* on our tree!"

"I know." Vanessa nodded "That means he's marking it as his territory."

Ricki scrunched up her nose. "Yuck! I'm going inside."

Vanessa scratched behind the dog's ears, gave the wavy fur on his back a few strokes, then said, "I'm going inside, too, to talk to Dad."

The dog dashed past her and Ricki up the porch steps. He sniffed the potted plants and the old wicker chairs, then plopped down right on the doormat. He stretched out, rested his chin on his paws, and sighed.

Vanessa smiled. "Gosh, he seems to belong here, doesn't he?"

Ricki looked at her sideways. "Wait a minute. Are you thinking what I think you're thinking?"

Vanessa shuffled her feet. "I think so."

"Oh, for Pete's sake." Ricki sighed. "Listen, this dog probably belongs to someone in the neighborhood."

Vanessa raised an eyebrow. "But what if he doesn't?"

Ricki stared down at the dog's shaggy black fur, his enormous, clumsy paws, and the soulful brown eyes gazing back at her. "I guess I had in mind something . . . *smaller* when you said you wanted a dog."

"But Ricki, he's perfect! Cute and sweet and protective. Did you see how he placed himself in front of us in the doorway of the spooky house?'' She gave him another scratch behind the ears. ''Come on, I'm going to tell Dad!''

Chapter Eight

Walking into the front hall, Vanessa and Ricki heard a trumpet whining out a long, sour note in the living room to the right. From the dining room to the left came loud hammering.

Ricki peeked in and found a chubby woman with short gray hair sitting cross-legged on top of the dining room table, which was covered by newspapers. She banged with a rubber mallet on what looked like a green clay bowling ball.

"Hi, Maureen," Vanessa said over Ricki's shoulder.

The woman looked up, holding the rubber mallet high. "Oh, hello, Vanessa. Ricki." She frowned and continued banging.

"Who is that?" Ricki whispered, following Vanessa across the hall to the living room.

"Don't you remember Maureen? She grew all the flowers for the bower at Dad and Anita's wedding."

"Oh, yeah." Ricki frowned. "What is she doing on the table?"

"She's a sculptor. Apparently, she's sculpting."

"Oh. On top of our dining room table?"

Vanessa shrugged. "I guess it's where she's most comfortable. Dad's artist friends have kind of odd work habits."

74

You can say that again, Ricki thought. The Shepherds' apartment used to look like a museum, every corner filled with strange-looking piles of driftwood, huge blotch-covered canvasses, and patches of sewn-together fabric that were supposed to be sculptures or paintings or hangings. Andy's friends counted on him to let them use his apartment for work space because their own places were too small, Vanessa had explained. Now, Ricki realized, they were going to be using Andy's house. Which now also happened to be *hers*.

Another note on the trumpet sirened through the air. Leaning against the windowsill in the living room stood Andy with his electric bass guitar. Gordon sat in a folding director's chair in front of the electric keyboard. A short, wiry-thin man stood between them, blowing into his trumpet. Ricki recognized him as Topp, a member of Fast Forward.

"You sure you want this kind of phrasing?" Topp asked, looking out of the corner of his eye at Andy and Gordon.

"Just give it a try." Andy grinned.

Topp shrugged and looked down at the sheet of music on his stand, then played another set of notes.

Vanessa walked quietly across the room to join her father. She crossed her arms and listened. It was always fun to hear her father's and Gordon's compositions being played for the first time, especially the unusual ones.

Ricki stayed in the doorway. She shifted from foot to foot and stuck her hands in her pockets. Topp kept making those weird sounds on the trumpet, which rang in Ricki's ears. Probably, if she put her hands over her ears, Topp's feelings would be hurt. Andy's and

75

Gordon's, too. Vanessa would definitely gripe about it later.

"Hey, I get it. That's hip," Topp said when he finished. Then he waved at Vanessa and Ricki. "How y'all doin'?"

Vanessa smiled. "That sounded great, Topp. Such a chromatic melody."

He nodded. "Leave it to your daddy and ol' Gord here to cook up somethin' so unexpected."

Chromatic melody? Ricki repeated to herself. What was that? She never understood more than three words or so of whatever Vanessa and her dad's pals talked about together. This music and art stuff was all a mystery to her and made her feel as if she had just landed on the planet. Or even worse, as if Vanessa were a grown-up and she were just a little kid.

Vanessa tugged on her father's sleeve. "Dad, can I ask you something? It's important."

Andy nodded. "Sure. We're due for a break, anyway. You guys want to help yourselves to the icebox? There's some mineral water in there for you, Gordon."

Topp and Gordon headed out. Andy rested his guitar against the wall.

Vanessa took a deep breath. "Um, well, Dad, could you look out the window, at the porch?"

"The window? Okay." He raised a brown eyebrow at her. "How come?"

"Just look." Vanessa could hardly keep still. Her cheeks flushed hot. She clasped her hands together as her father leaned out on the windowsill.

"What am I supposed to—Hey, who is that?"

Ricki left her post by the doorway and came to stand by Vanessa. "It's a dog," she informed him.

"I can see that." Andy whistled. "Hey, boy! Wow, he's good-looking, isn't he? Huge. Whose is he?"

Vanessa swallowed. "That's what I wanted to talk to you about. I mean, isn't he just perfect? He's really sweet and friendly and smart, too, and—"

Andy pulled himself back in through the window. Then he slipped his hands into his jeans pockets. "Vee, are you saying you want to keep this dog?"

"You said we could get a dog when things settled down here. And now you and Anita are back from the honeymoon and everything, so . . . " Vanessa saw the look on her father's face and stopped. Her heart sank.

His eyes drooped at the corners. "Vee, I've got to tell you something—something I learned while Anita and I were in Maine. I'm sorry I haven't told you before now." He sat in the armchair, feet planted wide apart, elbows resting on his knees. "On our honeymoon, a beautiful cocker spaniel from a nearby cabin used to wander onto our beach now and then, and Anita wouldn't go anywhere near it."

Vanessa's eyes lit up. "Oh, you mean she's afraid of dogs, like Ricki is? That's no problem. Even Ricki's starting to get used to *this* dog. He's really nice."

Andy shook his head. "Anita isn't afraid of dogs, Vee. I wish it were that simple. She's *allergic* to them."

Vanessa kept looking up at her father. She couldn't believe her ears. This just couldn't be! Dad had *promised* she could have a dog. And now there was a sweet, beautiful one right on the front porch. He couldn't say no!

But she knew that was exactly what he was saying. Her eyes clouded over with tears.

*   *   *

The next morning, Vanessa was the first one up. Just after dawn she slowly opened the living room window and peeked out.

The dog was still there.

Andy hadn't let Vanessa play with him all afternoon and evening the day before. He had even called Anita at work and told her to come in through the back door of the kitchen when she got home. If they just left the dog alone, Andy said, he'd wander back home.

But he hadn't. As far as Vanessa could tell, the poor thing hadn't budged from his spot on the doormat all night long.

Again, she felt tears sting her eyes. How awful it must be to be lost, hungry, and alone. Vanessa wanted to cuddle him and tell him everything would be all right. He'd probably appreciate a little breakfast, too.

Surely it wouldn't hurt just to say hi. If he was going to go home, he probably would have by now, wouldn't he?

Vanessa felt like a criminal as she crept down the hall toward the front door. She hardly ever disobeyed her father. Obeying him was usually easy, since he was more or less reasonable. This time, though . . .

The minute Vanessa's hand touched the doorknob she heard a loud thumping out on the porch. She opened the door to find the dog right in front of her, pushing his nose against the screen, tail going a mile a minute. When he saw her he let out a whine of delight and jumped up on the screen. His big front paws and huge shaggy head were right at Vanessa's eye level.

She giggled. "You silly thing. Get down, okay? You'll wake everyone."

The dog let his paws drop to the porch floor with a thud. He stood and watched her, tail still wagging.

"Oh, my, you're so cute." Vanessa sighed. "What are we going to do with you?"

As if wondering the same thing, the dog shifted eagerly from paw to paw.

"You want company, don't you?" Vanessa looked over her shoulder toward the stairs. No one was up yet. Surely it wouldn't hurt to go out and pet the poor creature for just a minute.

Twenty minutes later she was sitting on the top porch step, the dog spread out like a big black scruffy rug across her lap. He stretched his legs out luxuriously to let her scratch his belly.

Early sunlight sparkled off dewdrops all over the front yard, on the grass, the tree leaves, and the red and white petunias Andy and Anita had planted along the front path. Vanessa sighed. For that moment, at least, she felt very, very happy.

"Someone's in heaven." The voice came from behind the screen door.

Startled, Vanessa and the dog both whirled around to find Anita standing there.

Anita smiled. "Didn't mean to spook you two. You looked so peaceful, like something out of one of those old oil portraits of children with their faithful hounds."

Vanessa blushed. "I know I'm not supposed to be here, but he's so sweet. . . ."

"I know." Anita rubbed the sleeves of her bathrobe. "I know he is, honey. I'm so, so sorry. I wish we could—"

"It's okay," Vanessa interrupted. Her lower lip had

started to tremble. She didn't want Anita to say anything more.

"Oh, but honey, I truly am sorry." Anita leaned her forehead against the screen. "If there were any possible way . . . Well, I suppose the important thing is that we help this big guy find his home."

"I don't think he has one anymore. I mean, he seems . . . lost."

Anita sighed. "It's so sad. So many stray and abandoned pets. Andy said he has no tags on his collar."

Vanessa shook her head. "It looks like he's outgrowing the collar, too."

"Really? Well, we can probably fix that if there's room to put an extra notch in it. Why don't you unbuckle it for a minute and let me take a look?"

Vanessa gave the dog a scratch under the black nylon collar, unfastened its clasp, and got up to give it to Anita. He followed right at Vanessa's heels.

Anita backed into the hall, away from the door. "Sorry, big fella, I'm not getting near you. Last time I got close to a dog I was in bed for two days blowing my nose. Hold the collar up, hon, so I can see it. Yes, there's plenty of room for another notch. I can't touch it, but your dad can probably fix it. Oh, wait a minute. What's that, Vanessa?"

"What?" Vanessa peered at the collar.

"Look, is that a little metal plate there, on the underside of his collar?"

"It is!" Vanessa said. "Hey, there's writing on it! It—it says, 'Kirby.' And, 'Dr. Helen Chang,' and then a phone number."

Anita smiled at the dog, who wagged his tail in

return. "Looks like we may have found your home, Kirby. Well, Vanessa, shall we call the number?"

In the kitchen, Vanessa chewed on her cheek while Anita dialed. She wanted there to be an answer to the rings and for Dr. Chang to be a nice person with a big yard and a freezer full of T-bone steaks. On the other hand, she wanted Anita to hang up and announce that she had changed her mind. That Kirby was so adorable there was no way she could give him up, even if it meant wearing a gas mask all the time.

"Hello?" Anita said into the phone. "Oh, hello. Yes. My name is Anita Romero, and I think we've found your dog."

"I can't believe people are so cruel," Andy said, shaking his head. "To just dump a dog that way."

Ricki glanced across the dinner table at Vanessa, who hadn't said a word. She didn't even look up, but just poked at a leaf of lettuce with her fork. No one seemed to be very interested in eating dinner that night.

"It's unforgivable," said Anita in a quiet voice. She had a tight look around her eyes and mouth.

When Ricki had woken up that morning, the first thing she saw was Vanessa in bed, crying. Vanessa had told her through blubbery sobs that the dog's collar had a tag with his veterinarian's phone number on it. After Anita had phoned, the vet called the dog's home number and learned that his family had moved away and left no forwarding address. Sometimes, Dr. Chang had explained, people who move couldn't take pets with them, so they "dumped" them in neighborhoods, thinking they'd luck into a new home.

The best thing to do, according to Dr. Chang, was

to take the dog to the local animal shelter and hope that his owners came for him. If not, the vet had added, Kirby was a wonderful dog with a good chance of finding another home.

Ricki sighed. Poor Vee.

At the shelter that afternoon, she hadn't cried. Ricki and Andy stood beside her when the shelter worker took Kirby away into the kennels. It wasn't until they got home and Vanessa saw the doormat where Kirby had slept that a tear had sneaked out of her eye and dribbled down her cheek.

Ricki watched as Vanessa finally speared the lettuce leaf and forced it into her mouth.

Vanessa kept trying to remember what the shelter worker had said: Kirby would be happiest if his own family came for him. Or maybe a nice person with lots of T-bone steaks would adopt him, after all. Vanessa decided just to keep her fingers crossed and try not to get depressed.

Glancing around the dinner table, she suddenly felt a little better. She remembered a saying she had read somewhere. *Misery loves company*. Her father looked pale. Anita just pecked at her food. Even Ricki seemed quiet, although she had been the least enthusiastic about having a dog.

Misery loves company. Maybe, she thought, that was one thing families were for.

Chapter Nine

Ricki's left arm felt ready to fall off. Right in the doorway of her and Vanessa's room, she stopped and dropped the heavy dresser drawer she'd just carried upstairs.

"Oof! How can a few T-shirts weigh so much?" She leaned against the door frame, rubbing her arm.

Vanessa glanced at Ricki from her desk, where she was busy sketching out a floor plan for rearranging their room. "You're probably tired. We've been moving stuff all morning."

It was Saturday, four days after the trip to the animal shelter, and although Vanessa hadn't forgotten about Kirby the dog, she wasn't feeling quite so weepy about him anymore. The whole family seemed to have perked up, mostly because they were too busy to stay sad. The lease on the condo where Ricki and Anita had lived was ending Monday, so they had to finish moving out all their belongings. Also, Andy and Anita had taken Vanessa out for shakes yesterday at the Happy Carrot Health Café while Ricki had softball practice. She could tell they were trying to give her extra attention to help her feel better, and it worked.

She looked up from her desk and saw Ricki climbing

over the jungle of dresser drawers and packing boxes to her bed, where she shoved aside a pile of her camera gear and collapsed.

"What are you doing?" Vanessa asked.

"Going on strike." Ricki lay sprawled on her back, blue baseball cap half-covering her face. "Mom and Andy are slave drivers. They insist we get everything out of the condo today, so we can clean it tomorrow. Boy, won't that be fun!" She made a horrible face.

"You're not going to leave that drawer in the doorway, are you, Ricki?"

"Mmm-hmm." Ricki nodded. "I am."

"Ricki, there is stuff all over the place. This room is a disaster area. We have to decide where it'll all go."

Ricki opened one eye and glanced about. Vanessa had a point. Thanks to all Ricki's junk from the condo, the place was pretty messy, even by her own standards. They really did have to straighten it out.

She turned on her side and propped her head up on an elbow. "All right. Let's decide."

Vanessa picked her way carefully between an orange crate overflowing with old sneakers and Ricki's upside-down black metallic desk, which looked like a skeleton, emptied of its drawers. She cleared a little space at the foot of Ricki's bed and sat there cross-legged.

Watching Vanessa, Ricki thought of a finicky cat. Even the expression on Vanessa's delicate features looked prim and fussy, as if she could barely stand being in the middle of all that mess.

"Now," Vanessa began, frowning at the sheet of paper in her hand. "We can divide the room more or less in half, so that I'll have all my things on my side, and you'll have yours on yours. The problem is that it will be hard to do that because your dresser is so big, and it won't really fit on your side, so we'll have to put it here." Vanessa pointed at a pink rectangle on the sheet of paper. "See, all your things are drawn in pink felt tip, and all of mine are in green."

Ricki made a face. "I hate pink."

"Don't be silly. The dresser will go against the wall between the south windows. Our beds are here and here, one under each window. Our desks are against the wall on either side of the door. Of course it would be better to have the desks between the windows, to catch the light, but that's where your dresser has to go because it's so big."

"It's not that big," Ricki objected. "It's got six drawers, just like yours."

"Well, mine is tall, but yours is long, so it takes up more space. Now, I've got two bookshelf units, but I'll really need only one now, because I'm going to take a lot of the books I've already read down to the shelves in the den, so you can have the other one."

"I don't have many books."

Vanessa frowned. "Well, how about your softball and soccer trophies, and your framed photographs and camera stuff? You could put those on the shelves."

Ricki shrugged and stood up. "Okay. Sounds fine. Let's get going." She was starting to feel antsy. Vanessa was the kind of person who would sit around planning all day if you let her.

"Wait." Vanessa pointed at the floor plan. "You haven't seen the rest of the plan."

"I'm sure it's fine, Vee. Just fine. Let's get moving now, okay?"

Vanessa sighed. Ricki could be so impatient. She

always jumped right into things without a bit of planning.

"Here," Ricki said, "help me get this rocker out of the way, so I can start moving the dresser drawers."

Vanessa lifted one arm of her white wicker rocking chair, and Ricki got the other. Ricki headed toward the door. Vanessa headed toward the windows.

"Where are you going?" Vanessa asked.

"To the hall," said Ricki. "We can stick it out there and take it to the guest room or somewhere later."

"The guest room? That's my rocker. Why should it go to the guest room?"

Ricki shrugged. "Because it takes up too much space in here. It's already going to be crowded. What do we need a rocker for, anyway?"

"This is my rocker, Ricki. It does not take up too much space. Look, I've got it all mapped out here on the floor plan."

"I don't care about the floor plan. This chair is too big. Our desk chairs and beds give us plenty of places to sit." Ricki scratched her ear. "Plus, your rocker is old-looking."

"Old-looking?" Vanessa put a hand on her hip. "It's beautiful! I've taken very good care of it. My grandmother rocked my mother in it when she was a baby, and Mama rocked me in it, too."

"You're kidding!" Ricki shoved back the bill of her baseball cap. "Your *grandmother* used that chair with your mom? Then it's *really* old."

"That doesn't mean there's anything wrong with it." Vanessa raised an eyebrow.

"It's old-fashioned, Vee."

"So?"

"It'll look totally weird with my furniture," Ricki said.

"Well, it goes perfectly with mine." Vanessa started pulling on the chair again.

Ricki tugged back. "Keep it on your side of the room."

"You're being unreasonable, Ricki." Vanessa's chin jutted out. "It won't fit on my side. It has to go in the middle, between our beds."

Ricki sighed and flopped down on Vanessa's bed. "I don't really like old-fashioned stuff."

Lifting her eyebrow, Vanessa said, "Well, I don't like your dresser, either. Or your desk. They're black and too modern. They don't have any character."

"They have plenty of character," Ricki countered.

"I disagree, but we're just going to have to compromise, aren't we? Your dresser has to go in the middle and so docs my chair."

Ricki sighed again. Although she hated to give in, she knew Vanessa was right about the compromising part. Rolling her eyes, she got up.

They moved the chair to the middle of the room.

That evening at dinner, Anita smiled at them and Andy. "I'd like to officially thank you all for the hard work moving everything today. *And* apologize in advance for all the hard work I'm going to make you do tomorrow."

"Here, here!" Andy agreed. "That deserves a toast!"

They all raised the fancy, long-stemmed goblets of lemonade that Anita had set the table with and clinked them together, laughing.

"This is a night to celebrate," Anita said.

Ricki took a bite of broccoli cheese casserole. "Celebrate what?"

"Oh, just this." Anita waved a hand around the table. "Us. The move. Being all together."

Vanessa giggled. "Finally." She looked at Ricki to share a secret smile.

Their smiles grew bigger when they saw Andy reach over to twine his fingers with Anita's on the table. *They* looked at each other and beamed.

Ricki giggled.

"Speaking of the move," Andy said, "and being all together, how's it going in your room, girls?"

Ricki took another bite of the casserole, chewing hard. It had lots of little nuggets and grainy things in it. Most of the stuff Andy cooked was good, but she wished he wouldn't put so many seeds and nuts in everything, even though he said it added valuable protein for her sports activities. All Ricki knew was that it took a long time to chew dinner these days.

"Our room is fine," Vanessa was saying. "We're organizing it."

Andy looked at Ricki. "Need a hand moving your furniture around?"

Ricki shrugged. "Not really."

"We'd be glad to help," Anita said.

Ricki glanced at her out of the corner of her eye. Her mom's tone of voice was kind of funny. Firm. Too firm, as if she were about to *insist* on helping.

"We have a confession to make," Andy said, taking a roll from the bread basket. "We overheard your, um, discussion earlier today, girls."

Ricki aimed the corner of her eye at him. "Which discussion?"

"The one," answered Anita, "about how to arrange your room."

"Anita and I have been thinking. . . . It might be better if you two had separate rooms." Andy smiled cheerfully.

"Separate rooms!" Vanessa's eyebrows shot upward.

Ricki's eyes went wide. "We don't want separate rooms!"

"There's no reason why one of you shouldn't take the guest room," Anita said, calmly sipping lemonade.

"The guest room? That's for guests!" Vanessa exclaimed.

"Well, within the year I'll have converted the attic into living space, and we can use that for guests," said Andy.

"In any case," Anita continued, "maybe you should think about that guest room."

Ricki scrunched up her nose. Vanessa pursed her lips. The very idea of having separate rooms horrified them. The whole reason they had wanted to become sisters was to be together!

"We don't want to move," Ricki announced.

Vanessa shook her head. "Absolutely not. We're very happy, just where we are."

Andy stroked his beard. "Hmm. Well, if you should change your minds . . ."

"No way!" the girls chimed in unison.

Anita glanced at Andy over the rim of her goblet. Andy shrugged.

From the looks on their parents' faces, the girls could tell that they hadn't heard the last of the separate rooms idea.

"Well," Anita said, "how about dessert? I picked

up a surprise on the way home." From the kitchen she brought a little pink box crowded with dainty cream pastries.

After gobbling up three of them, Ricki patted her belly. "I'm stuffed. Can't move."

"So am I." Anita smiled. "Did you like yours, Vanessa?"

Licking chocolate off her lips, Vanessa nodded. "Mmm-hmm!"

"I can tell it's going to be hard to keep a waistline with *you* around," Andy said, shooting a fake glare at Anita. Then he got up to clear the dishes.

"Oh, honey, those can wait, can't they?" Anita asked.

Andy kept piling the dishes up. "Well, the problem is that food sticks to the plates, you know, and then they're tough to clean."

"So?" Anita shrugged and smiled. "No big deal, is it? Why don't we all go into the den and relax for a while?"

"It's hard for me to relax," Andy said, "with a mess like this sitting here. I know it doesn't bother you, but—"

"Well, of course it doesn't bother me, honey. These are just dirty plates, not nuclear bombs."

Andy gathered up the napkins, grinning again. "Did you ever give some thought to your name, Anita? Break it up a little bit, and you know how it works out?"

Anita gave him a sideways look. "No. How?"

"Well . . . A-nita. Get it? As in, the word 'neat'? Putting the prefix 'a' in front of a word makes it mean the opposite, right? So, get it? A-*neata?* Not-neata?"

She kept looking at him sideways, without answering.

Then Ricki noticed a very slight narrowing of her mother's eyes and two bright spots of color on her high cheekbones. Ricki held her breath.

"Well, then *your* name," Anita said, "should be 'Super Neato,' shouldn't it? If you can't stand to leave dishes waiting for a few minutes."

"Dishes, laundry, old newspapers," Andy listed. "Right, I don't like to leave them lying around. Especially not for days, which seems to be your preference."

Vanessa chewed on her cheek. Her father's tone of voice was just a little too sharp. His eyes were getting that blank look in them—the one they got when he was angry. She looked at Ricki, who was biting a thumbnail.

They had to do something.

Ricki stood up. "Well let's get started on these dishes, huh?"

Vanessa almost fell over. *Ricki,* offering to start cleaning? Miracle! Anyway, it seemed to work on Andy and Anita. They were so surprised that, for the moment, they stopped arguing.

On Ricki's way to the kitchen, she heard her mother sigh. Anita got up and reached for the casserole dish and the salad bowl. Soon they were all in the kitchen, silently working.

Ricki thought of a movie she had seen about a family huddling in a farmhouse in the eye of a hurricane. The winds and rain of half the storm had just finished whipping at their house, but in the eye it was eerily calm. Now they had to wait for the other half of the storm to hit.

Instead, the doorbell rang.

"That must be Bernard," said Andy. "He wants to use the den tonight."

"The den?" Anita asked. "What for?"

"He's got a spot in the Arts Fair at the university next month. I think he's carving another totem pole."

"Oh." Anita nodded, scraping a plate into the garbage.

Andy peered at her. "Why are you making that face?"

"Which face?"

Ricki and Vanessa had been trying not to look at their parents, but now they couldn't help it. They peered at Anita, too.

"The one," replied Andy, "where you kind of narrow your eyes."

Anita shrugged. "It's just interesting that you don't mind Bernard or Maureen or any of your other friends making a mess. Plus, I was hoping *we* could use the den tonight."

"Well, first of all," said Andy, "Bernard and Maureen and the others clean up after themselves. And second, I thought we could sit in the living room tonight."

Anita shrugged again. "Fine."

This was awful. The girls hated hearing their parents argue. It always seemed that the Sisters Scheme was about to backfire. Add that to their own arguments, and it felt as if the Sisters Scheme was turning into the Sisters War!

Vanessa kept chewing on her cheek. Ricki fidgeted. When Andy came back after showing Bernard into the den, the girls feared the worst. He dipped his hands into the sink's soapy water to scrub the dishes Anita had scraped.

Anita tapped her long, plum-painted fingernails on

the counter beside him. "Andy, hon, what do you have against the dishwasher?"

Ricki and Vanessa held their breaths. Not again!

"Well, I know it's ridiculous." Andy shrugged. "But I'm used to hand washing. Never had a dishwasher before. When I installed this one, I thought, great! No more soapy mess. But, well, here I am. . . ."

Anita chuckled. "Old habits die hard, don't they? Well, how about we just establish a new tradition?" She took the plate from Andy's hand, opened the dishwasher door, and slid it in. "Voilà!"

"Here, I'll put one in, too," Vanessa said quickly. Maybe if they kept this on a light note . . .

Andy shook his head, grinning. "Looks like I'm outnumbered."

"Three to one!" Ricki slipped in another plate.

Then, she and Anita put away the leftovers while Vanessa and Andy finished with the dishes.

"Vanessa," Anita said when they turned out the kitchen lights, "do you want to look through the aquarium catalogs tonight?"

"Sure!" Vanessa answered in delight. They had made it through the whole hour without another argument. "Oh, but I need to practice cello first."

Anita put an arm around Vanessa and patted her shoulder. "Sounds good. I'll be in the den—I mean the living room—reading, whenever you're ready."

"Okay. I'll come down in about an hour." Vanessa ran upstairs, ponytail flying behind her. No aquarium could replace wonderful Kirby the dog, but it was exciting to have *some* new pets on the way. Anita and Dad had promised her a big saltwater tank.

On the living room sofa, Ricki collapsed and picked

up the TV remote control. She felt nearly exhausted. Keeping parents out of arguments was hard work!

She was just about to punch on the TV when her mother tugged the control box out of her hand.

"Uh-uh," Anita said, sitting down next to her on the sofa. "Please, honey, no TV tonight. Let's have a quiet evening together."

"Together? You're just going to read, Mom. And Andy's looking over music sheets or something."

"Actually, it's a piece for the Surreal Sound concert next month," Andy said, grinning at her from the armchair.

"See? You guys are both busy," Ricki told her mother.

"Exactly. Which is why we don't want the boob tube chattering at us."

Ricki sighed. It wasn't fair. No one seemed to care about her or what *she* wanted these days. Vanessa, on the other hand, had been getting all kinds of special treatment from Anita and Andy because of Kirby. Anita was going to buy Vanessa an aquarium, and those were expensive. She was going to take Vanessa shopping for it and help her put it together and everything. Anita hadn't taken Ricki shopping in months! Well, weeks, at least. And now they wouldn't even let Ricki watch TV. She reached for the newspaper and flung it open to the comics.

The sound of Vanessa's cello came wafting downstairs. First, Ricki heard some long, smooth notes that sort of went up and down in a nice way. But then Vanessa started playing short, fast notes up and down, over and over, to the point where Ricki thought she'd go crazy. Vanessa played that same darn thing every day. Ricki stuck her fingers in her ears.

"Driving you bananas?" she heard Andy ask though her finger plugs.

Ricki nodded.

He grinned. "I know. Eventually you get used to it, but in the meantime it can be maddening. How about if I go up and shut her door? Then we won't hear it as strongly."

He bounded upstairs and came back a minute later. "Better now?"

Ricki nodded. "Much. Why does she have to do that?"

"You mean, practice scales? Well, they're like exercises in music. Scales are very important for finger strength, among other things."

Ricki shook her head. "I could never do that. I'd go nuts."

"It seems that way. But you'd be surprised. You might even like it if you got into it."

"No way!" Ricki shook her head. "I'm no good at music. Can't even hum on key."

Andy laughed. "Hey, come on. You're good at sports, aren't you?"

"What does that have to do with music?" Ricki asked, grinning. "So what if I can hit a softball or kick a soccer ball?"

Andy stroked his beard. "Well, sports teach self-discipline and the value of practice. Those are things you need as a musician, too. You also need some physical strength and agility, believe it or not, just like in sports."

"Really?"

"Really." Andy nodded. "Want me to show you?" He picked up his guitar. "See, on this chord—it's a G-13—I need to be able to stretch my fingers all the way from the little finger on the B string to the index finger on the low E string."

"Wow." Ricki sat forward. "That looks pretty hard."

"It is, at first, but not after you practice for a while. Here, try it."

Ricki went quiet as Andy handed her his guitar, then helped her position it on her knees. She had never held a real guitar before, and definitely not *Andy's* guitar. His instruments and audio equipment had always seemed off limits.

In just a couple of minutes he showed Ricki how to relax her hand so that the fingers limbered up and stretched easily.

Ricki strummed. A broken-up, sour sound came from the guitar. She laughed.

Anita smiled at her over the tops of her reading glasses.

"Did you hear that? I played the guitar!"

"I certainly did hear." Anita nodded. "Bravo."

"Now *that* was a difficult chord," Andy said, "but you played it. If you can do that one, you can handle the more basic ones."

"Like which?" Ricki asked.

"Here's a D major chord." He helped her reposition her fingers.

Trudging downstairs, Vanessa felt tired. The whole day of moving boxes and furniture had taken its toll. At the moment, she felt a little hurt, too. Why had her father closed the door to her room while she was practicing? He had never done that before. She thought he liked listening to her practice.

Vanessa walked into the living room, ready to ask him about it. But before she could say anything, she heard Ricki laughing. Then she saw Ricki strumming Andy's guitar and Andy nodding his head with the beat.

"Dad—" Vanessa began.

He didn't seem to hear.

"Dad, I was wondering—"

"Just a minute, Vee," he said, without even looking at her.

Vanessa felt a funny tightness in her throat. She frowned. It was silly, really silly, to feel this way. But she couldn't help it. Seeing Dad so focused on Ricki, and ignoring *her,* his own daughter. . . . She was actually jealous over him, for the very first time in her life.

Chapter Ten

The girls hardly spoke to each other as they got ready for bed. It had been a long day. Tomorrow might be even longer. Their parents had already come up with a list of all the cleanup chores that had to be done at the condo. Mopping the kitchen floor, scrubbing the bath tile, dusting the window blinds.

Cleaning would take forever, Ricki thought mopily. A lot of the chores had probably been Andy's idea. She and her mother never dusted the blinds.

Vanessa didn't mind cleaning. It could even be fun sometimes, if you had a system. But she did mind having to clean Ricki and Anita's mess, because if only they had been better housekeepers while they lived in the condo, there wouldn't be a mess to clean now.

"Good-night," she mumbled when she fell into bed.

"Night," Ricki mumbled back.

Both girls slipped into sleep almost right away.

Just minutes later, Vanessa woke up. "Ricki, stop snoring!"

"For Pete's sake, Vee, I wasn't snoring! Why'd you wake me up?"

"Hush!" Vanessa whispered.

"You wake me up, then tell me to hush?"

"Listen!" Vanessa ordered.

Then Ricki heard it, too. Snoring. Deep, grumbly snoring.

"He's back!" whispered Vanessa. "Emmett!"

Ricki sat up to listen better. "Either him or your dad. It sounds like a man."

"Dad never snores." Vanessa shook her head. "Let's go tell him!"

"Tell him what? He and Mom never believe us."

"Well, they'll have to this time!"

"Wait, Vee. They must have already heard it. I mean, Aunt Allegra is hard of hearing, but they're not."

Vanessa nodded. "You're right. This is really loud, and it's right in the hall. They've got to hear it."

At any moment, Vanessa thought, there would be her father's familiar step out in the hall. Then he'd call, "Vanessa? Ricki? You girls okay in there?"

In a wink, Ricki kept telling herself, her mother would be at her side, holding her hand, and apologizing for not having believed them earlier.

The snoring went on. Gradually, it grew softer.

"It's going away!" Ricki whispered.

After a moment, the snoring faded completely.

"It's gone!" whispered Vanessa. "Why haven't our parents come to check on us?"

"Maybe they're scared," Ricki suggested.

"So am I," Vanessa confessed. "Even though, I don't know, it's funny to hear a ghost snore."

Ricki giggled. "Yeah, it kind of is. I guess Emmett sleeps, too."

"I wonder if he dreams." Vanessa snuggled under the covers. "Let's not get up, Ricki. If our parents heard it, I'm sure they'll investigate, but if they didn't, let's just—"

"Stay tucked in bed?" Ricki asked. "Safe and cozy?"

"Exactly," Vanessa answered, pulling the covers over her head.

"Fine with me." Ricki wasn't about to admit it, but having Vanessa around sure could be fun, even when they were both being scaredy cats.

Vanessa sighed and closed her eyes, happy that she had a sister like Ricki to share a ghost with, even if it meant having to share a father, too.

"See, girls? Ain't nobody up here but us chickens." Andy shone a huge flashlight all over the attic floorboards. Its bright ray cast weird shadows across the bare wood walls and heavy-beamed ceiling.

The girls were not convinced.

"If we had a ghost," Andy said, "wouldn't it make sense for it to live in the attic? And it's not here, is it?"

"The ghost is a *he*, Dad, not an 'it,' " Vanessa corrected.

"And we don't know that he lives in the attic," added Ricki. "Whenever we hear him, it sounds like he's in the hall."

With his shirt sleeve, Andy dusted cobwebs off the sill of the big room's one window and sat on it. "Come on, you two. You don't really and truly believe in— what's his name? Ernest? You're just having some summer fun, right?"

Vanessa pursed her lips. "Emmett."

"We heard him, Andy. It's kind of hard not to

believe in him after you hear him moaning and groaning and snoring," Ricki said.

"Not to mention chasing us down the hall!" Vanessa put in. "We are *not* just two bored little girls having 'summer fun,' as you call it."

"I don't get how come you and Mom didn't hear him snoring last night." Ricki frowned.

"My question exactly," said Andy. "If Emmett was so loud, right out there in the hall, how come Anita and I didn't hear him? Our room is just at the other end."

Vanessa shrugged. "Heavy sleepers."

"I am," her father agreed. "But Anita isn't."

"You don't believe us, then." Vanessa crossed her arms. "I knew it."

"We do believe you, Vee. Honestly." He came over and squatted before the girls. "But we believe there's some logical explanation for this. Something is making those noises, and for some reason they're only audible from your room."

"An explanation like what?" Ricki asked.

Andy shrugged. "Could be anything, I guess. The wind, for instance."

"That's what we thought at first." Vanessa sighed.

Andy chuckled. "Listen, I don't doubt that this is very puzzling to you. Even scary, right?"

Ricki and Vanessa nodded.

"And I'm sorry if Anita and I have seemed, oh, disbelieving or casual about the whole thing. I apologize." He held up his hand like a Boy Scout. "I hereby promise to be more serious and try to get to the bottom of things. For starters, today I'm going to keep the promise I made before. I'll call Pierre, the guy who

101

sold me the house, to see if he has any idea of who the earlier owners were and where Clementine may be these days. How's that?''

Ricki clapped her hands. ''Great!''

''I'll also start fixing up this room.'' Andy stood up and cast about the attic with the flashlight again. ''There's no reason why we shouldn't be able to use this space for guests.'' He scratched his beard.

Ricki and Vanessa looked at each other. Just as they suspected, Anita and Andy had not yet given up on the separate rooms idea.

''Plus,'' Andy went on, ''if those noises are somehow coming from up here, I might discover their source while remodeling. Now what do you say we boogie downstairs for lunch?'' He rested a hand on each girl's shoulder, then lit the way for them to climb down the narrow stairway.

Emmett was quiet the rest of the week. Andy kept trying to call his friend but never got through. The girls didn't have much time to think about Emmett or Clementine, anyway, because Ricki was busy with the second summer session of softball, and on Friday Anita took Vanessa to buy her aquarium.

Ricki watched them setting it up in the den Saturday morning.

''Will you check on the mail, honey?'' Anita asked her. ''I'm expecting a deposit refund from the condo manager.''

When Ricki came back she was waving an envelope.

''The refund?'' Anita asked eagerly.

''Nope, it's for Vee and me! From Aunt Allegra.''

The girls tore the envelope open. They read silently.

My dears,

Just a little note to thank you and your parents' again for my lovely stay with you.

Also, I wish to report some information that may be of use. I have spoken with my neighbor Flora Carlson on your situation regarding Mr. Emmett Tibbs and Miss Clementine Hewitt. Flora suggests that if you are disturbed by a spirit's activities, a possible remedy is to assist him or her in feeling more at home. Emmett may be a bit off balance these days because of all the changes in the house, the remodeling and such, not to mention the presence of four new residents. Flora suggests you read aloud his letters to Miss Clementine, in a respectful manner, of course, to give him a greater sense of familiarity and a bit of reminiscence.

I talked also with Mr. Hauptman the grocer, and he agrees this is sound advice.

Please let me know how it works out.

And don't forget your teeth.

Missing you terribly. With all my love,

Allegra Reginald.

"Well?" asked Anita. "What does she say?"

"She misses us," said Vanessa.

"And we get to read the letters! Yippee!" Ricki whooped.

"The letters from Emmett to Clementine?" Anita asked. "Those would be fascinating. Dated 1936, right? I'd say they might even be historically valuable. But why does Aunt Allegra say you should read them?"

Vanessa frowned. "She says it will make Emmett

feel more at home. But I don't know. They're still Clementine's letters.''

"To make Emmett feel more at home?'' Anita shook her head at the girls. "For heaven's sake, you don't really—''

Ricki interrupted. "Aunt Allegra's neighbor, who has all the ghosts, says ours is probably upset because of all the remodeling and stuff, and because we're a new family here, so we have to help him feel more familiar with things.''

"Oh, for heaven's sake,'' Anita repeated. She rested her forehead against two fingers. "Sweeties, we don't have a ghost. Really, now. Aunt Allegra and her friends have their own ways of looking at things, but on this particular matter they're off the mark. I'm sure Emmett Tibbs and Clementine Hewitt actually lived and so forth, but as far as ghosts go—''

The phone on the desk rang and startled Anita so that she jumped about a foot. The girls giggled. Maybe Anita did halfway believe in Emmett, even if she wouldn't admit it.

"Uh, hello?'' she said, putting a hand on her chest to regain her composure.

"Come on, Vee,'' Ricki whispered. "Aunt Allegra says we should read the letters. Let's go get them.''

Ricki didn't hear Vanessa's reply, because her ears suddenly tuned in on her mother.

"Yes, uh, well, oh, fine,'' Anita was saying. "Just fine, thank you. Uh, pardon me? Oh, certainly. Yes. Of course.'' Her tone of voice was the high-pitched, too-polite one that she only used when she was either on the verge of being upset or trying very hard to impress someone. Or both.

"Vanessa, it's for you."

"For me?" Vanessa asked. "Wow, a letter and a phone call on the same day! Is it my grandparents?"

Anita shook her head. She put her palm over the phone mouthpiece and looked softly into Vanessa's eyes. "Hon, it's your mother."

Chapter Eleven

Vanessa's stomach turned a flip. "It's Mama?" she whispered.

Anita nodded and held the phone out to her.

Vanessa slowly put the receiver against her ear. "Hello?"

"Oh, darling, darling! How are you?" The voice was smooth and bright and pretty. Mama's voice. Vanessa hadn't heard it in almost a year.

"Hi, Mama! I'm fine. Where are you?" Vanessa noticed Ricki and Anita quietly leaving the room.

A laugh, light and high, came from the other end of the phone line. "In Hawaii, darling, still. A hotel here in Waikiki offered me a three-month singing engagement. I'm a hit here, you know."

"Nona sent me an article about you from a Hawaii newspaper," Vanessa said. "They called you a 'nightingale.' "

"Mother sent you that? Really?" Another laugh. "Well, love, now I have a surprise for you. My contract ends in August. What if I come to see you then?"

"In August? That's just—That's just a week away." Vanessa chewed on her cheek.

"I'd come in late August, but that's still not far off. Wouldn't it be lovely? I haven't seen you in, oh, how long has it been, darling? A year?"

"A year and a half," answered Vanessa. "The last time you came was two Easters ago."

"Yes, that's right. Much too long. I do miss you, love. Do you miss me?"

Vanessa nodded, fighting down the lump in her throat. "Yes, Mama."

"Then it's settled. I'm not certain of the exact date yet, but I'll buy my plane tickets soon and give you another call during the coming weeks. How does that sound?"

"Great! I-I have a lot to tell you about. I've grown a little. I'm four foot ten and three-quarters now. My hair is longer. Last summer Ricki and I made a pact not to cut our hair. It's down past our shoulders now. We hoped maybe we'd look like twins, but it really is hopeless because her hair is black and mine is—"

"How fun," Mama interrupted. "Well, darling, I'm sorry, but I have to run now. I'm late for a dress fitting. It's amazing how many I wear out just standing on a stage singing! Good-bye, now. We'll talk again soon, all right?"

" 'Bye, Mama." Vanessa swallowed hard when she heard the phone line click. She wished the call had lasted longer—much longer. Talking to Mama sometimes seemed like riding a roller coaster. It went up and down, and you never quite knew where it would stop. You always felt breathless afterward, but you wanted to go again.

Ricki peeked in around the door. "Are you through talking with your mom?"

Vanessa nodded.

"Well, what did she say?" Ricki asked eagerly.

Vanessa tried to act casual. "Oh, she's got a three-month singing contract at a hotel in Hawaii."

"Wow! Really? That's cool. She's getting famous!"

Vanessa nodded again. She knew Ricki was impressed by the glamorous pictures she'd seen of Mama.

"Well, what else did she say?" Ricki asked. "Does she swim and surf all day long, while she's not singing? Does she sail around with other famous people on their yachts?"

There was a funny look on Vanessa's face. Ricki didn't understand it. Vee's eyes were half-shut, as if she wasn't paying attention. And now her lower lip trembled.

"Vee, what . . . what's wrong?"

Vanessa shook her head. "Nothing." Her voice was small and shaky.

Ricki peered at her closely. "Something about your mom? Is she . . . okay?"

Vanessa nodded. "Fine. She's . . . she's coming to visit at the end of August."

"Wow! Really? Here, in Berkeley? That's great! Isn't it? I mean, don't you think it's great?"

Vanessa shrugged. "I just . . . it's been so long since I last saw her. I . . . oh, I want to see her, but at the same time I'm worried that I won't even recognize her or something. I mean, we don't really know each other anymore."

Ricki put an arm around her friend's shoulders. "Oh. I think I get it. I mean, if my father was still alive but I only saw him once a year or so, that would be weird." She sighed. "Hey, but you know what? You've got a whole month to get used to the idea, right? In the meantime you'll probably talk with her on the phone again, too."

Vanessa nodded.

"Probably the minute you see her you'll forget all about being nervous. Come on, stop worrying." Ricki patted Vanessa's arm. "Let's go tell Mom and Andy, okay?"

Walking out of the room with Vanessa, Ricki decided not to bug her about the letters just yet.

Sunday morning Vanessa got up a little after eight and found Anita already in the kitchen, drinking coffee and reading the paper.

"Good morning, Vanessa."

Anita looked unusually bright and cheerful. Nothing like she did on weekday mornings, when she dashed around like mad, always on the edge of being late. On weekends, she was more relaxed. Vanessa liked spending early Sunday mornings with her new stepmother. Andy often slept late after his Saturday night band gigs. Before he and Anita got married, Vanessa would just stay in bed reading, sometimes for hours after she awoke, not wanting to get up and be alone.

Today, she noticed Anita's smile was bigger than on most Sunday mornings.

"Did you hear the phone ring a while ago?" Anita asked.

"The phone?" Vanessa shook her head. Her heart started to beat faster. Mama again?

Swirling a spoon in her coffee, Anita smiled even bigger. "Every day *I've* been making a certain phone call, hon. I haven't told you about it because your father and I, well, we felt it might be better not to bring the subject up again, but today someone called me with such good news that I just have to tell you."

Vanessa frowned, completely baffled.

"It's about Kirby," Anita began, smiling up at Vanessa. "He's been adopted."

Vanessa almost jumped out of her chair. "Adopted!"

Anita laughed. "You look exactly like I did when I heard. Every day I've been calling the shelter to ask if anyone had come for him yet, and every day that passed I got more and more worried, because, well . . . they can't keep unwanted dogs there forever, and eventually . . ."

Vanessa swallowed, glad that Anita didn't finish the sentence. She already knew what happened to unwanted pets. "A necessary evil," Andy had called it. Unclaimed, unadopted pets had to be put to sleep.

"Anyway, I couldn't handle the idea of *that* happening to Kirby," Anita went on, "so I kept checking on him, and finally, today, I got a call from a woman named Shelley Kahn. She fosters dogs from the shelter, takes them on until another home can be found for them. She fell in love with Kirby at first sight, and she's going to do her best to find him a new home. Isn't that fabulous?"

"Oh, yes! I wish—" Vanessa caught herself just in time.

"I do, too, honey. I do, too. I'm awfully sorry

Kirby can't live with us. He's kind of special, isn't he?''

Vanessa nodded, fighting back a sniffle. "You can't help it if you have allergies.''

Anita sighed. "I guess it'll just have to be fish for this family, huh?''

Vanessa took one look at Anita's grim expression and couldn't help laughing. "I guess so.''

"Well, speaking of which, why don't you have some breakfast so we can go to the den and work on that good ol' aquarium?''

An hour later, Ricki finally dragged herself downstairs, followed soon after by Andy. The two of them made French toast, then wandered into the living room, where Andy talked Ricki into another guitar lesson.

Vanessa could hear them in the living room, laughing and strumming out chord after chord. Anita handed her a section of air hose to plant in the aquarium gravel. To Vanessa it still felt kind of strange to hear her father paying so much attention to *another* daughter, but it felt much less strange than it had a couple of weeks ago. After all, being sisters meant sharing, didn't it? Vanessa had just never had to share her dad before.

In the afternoon, Anita and Andy went up to the attic to plan the remodeling, while the girls put some finishing touches on their room.

"Isn't this a great day?'' asked Ricki. She stood on her bed, thumbtacks in one hand and a new poster in the other.

"It's awfully warm.'' Vanessa blew upwards at her bangs as she searched through a dresser drawer.

"No, I mean *this*," Ricki said. "Us. My mom and your dad, you know, all of us together doing family-type stuff. Home improvement and everything."

Vanessa gave Ricki a small smile. "Happy ending for the Sisters Scheme." She went back to frowning as she searched through another drawer. Ricki tried hanging the poster at different angles over the wall above her bed.

Beads of sweat gathered under Vanessa's bangs. She blew at them again and finally grabbed a plastic headband off her dresser top to hold them back.

"Ricki, have you seen my crocheted shawl?" Vanessa fanned herself with a hand. It was so darned hot.

"Your what? Oh, that lace thing?" Ricki turned the poster to a new angle. "It kept falling off your rocking chair."

"I know. I was going to drape it so it wouldn't, but now I can't find it."

"Oh. I put it in the closet." Ricki squinted at the poster, a photo of an all-woman rock band wearing lots of black leather, black eye makeup, and frizzy purple hair. Not a good match against the pink wall, Ricki decided. Come to think of it, she couldn't stand anything prissy pink.

"You did *what*?" Vanessa asked.

"Hmm?" Ricki was still squinting at the poster. "Oh, I hung your shawl thing in the closet. To get it out of the way."

"Out of the way?" Vanessa blinked. "Of what?"

"It looked funny. It was always falling to the floor right in the middle of things, so I hung it up."

Vanessa headed for her half of the closet. "Just

like that? You didn't even think to tell me about it? I just spent twenty minutes looking for it."

"Really?" Ricki decided she not only couldn't stand pale pink, she hated it. "Hey, Vee. Let's paint our room."

"What?" Vanessa finally found her shawl. Mrs. Quan, who was like a substitute grandmother, had made it for her as a going-away present when she and her dad moved out of the duplex. "Did you say paint something?"

"Our room," Ricki repeated. "Let's get a new color in here."

"This *is* a new color," said Vanessa, draping the shawl over the back of her rocker. "Dad and I painted it just before we moved in."

"It's gross." Ricki scrunched up her nose.

"Gross?" Vanessa's eyebrows flew upward. "It's very fresh-looking. I chose it myself."

"Well, how about if *I* get to choose something in here? You've got *your* paint, *your* curtains, *your* rug. . . ."

"But they look so nice."

"Yeah," said Ricki, "if you're a little girl."

"What do you mean?" Vanessa's cheeks, already flushed from the summer heat, grew even warmer.

"Everything is so old-fashioned in here," Ricki said. "Like kid stuff. You know, all frilly. Those lacy white curtains—"

"Suzanne helped me make those."

"And the flowery rug."

"My grandmother sent me that. It's an antique."

"Your comforter has got so many ruffles, I don't know why you don't get tangled up at night."

Vanessa put a hand on her hip and tapped one foot. "Ricki, do you have a point to make?"

"Yeah. I'm sick of all this lace and ruffles stuff. And that shawl thing looks really goofy when you put it on your rocker. Why do you do that?"

"It looks nice," Vanessa said. "You're supposed to drape shawls over things."

Ricki rolled her eyes. "It looks goofy."

"Have you ever thought," Vanessa began, "that some of *your* things might look goofy? Does *purple hair* strike you as just a little, tiny bit goofy?"

"Huh?" Ricki squinted at Vanessa, then at her poster. "Oh. Well, so what? Lots of people have purple hair these days. It's in style."

"It looks ridiculous."

"No, it doesn't," Ricki objected. "This poster came with the music tape I got. It's cool."

"You call that cool?" Vanessa pointed at the poster. "I would have nightmares with *her* standing over my bed."

Ricki turned her back to Vanessa and pushed in another thumbtack. "Right. Eleven-year-olds *do* have nightmares, don't they?"

"Don't start that again, Ricki. Just because you turned twelve two months before I will doesn't give you a right to—"

"Well, just because you were in this room two months before I was," Ricki interrupted, "doesn't give *you* a right to boss me."

"I'm not bossing you."

"Yes, you are. You want all your stuff to take over the room. The minute I put up something of my own, you say it looks ridiculous."

114

"You criticized my things first," Vanessa shot back. "You said it looks like a little girl's room."

"It does. And you might as well not even *live* in it, you keep it so neat. If one little ruffle is out of place, you have to smooth it out. It drives me nuts!"

Vanessa pursed her lips. "Well, you drive *me* nuts. I try not to even look at your side of the room, it's so messy."

"Yeah, I bet you wish I wasn't here. All you do is bug me. This doesn't even seem like my room. I feel like a visitor. I have to tiptoe around when you're practicing cello and—"

"You, tiptoe? Hah! I'm sure!" Vanessa gave a fake little laugh.

That was the last straw. Ricki jumped off the bed, tossed her handful of thumbtacks into an open desk drawer, and stomped to the door. She flung it wide and was about to slam it behind her when she heard voices.

Vanessa heard them, too. Loud voices, coming from the attic.

Halfway through the doorway, Ricki stopped to listen.

Vanessa held her breath.

The voices belonged to Andy and Anita.

They were absolutely, positively, without a doubt, yelling.

Chapter Twelve

"It's worn out, Andy," Anita yelled. "It's an old, tired joke now."

"You don't have to get upset," Andy yelled back. "It's just a joke."

"Yes, but you've run it into the ground. If you call me A-Neata one more time—"

"But it's funny," Andy interrupted. "You've got to admit, it fits."

"See what I mean? You just won't let it drop."

"Sure I will."

The girls heard a loud *thunk* on the ceiling above their heads. It sounded like a hammer falling on the attic floor.

"See? I let it drop," Andy said.

"You think you're funny, I guess," said Anita.

The girls heard her brisk footsteps clipping across the floor above them.

Then Andy asked, "Where are you going?"

"I hate it when you're in this sarcastic mood," Anita said. "I've had enough."

Her footsteps started down the stairs, with Andy's right behind them.

Ricki bit her lip. Vanessa chewed on her cheek.

116

In seconds their parents descended the attic stairway and stood at the far end of the hall, facing each other.

"I wish you wouldn't storm away when we have disagreements," Andy said.

"You're so impossible, what choice do I have?" countered Anita.

"Stay and talk. Work things out."

"When you're in a more cooperative mood, we'll talk." Anita crossed her arms and turned away from him.

Ricki ducked back through the doorway to the bedroom and almost ran into Vanessa. "Oh, sorry!" she whispered.

"It's okay," Vanessa answered.

The two of them hid behind the door, peering around it at their parents.

"In the meantime," Andy said, "we won't get anything settled."

"We don't settle anything when you pick on me, either." Anita recrossed her arms.

"Gosh!" Vanessa gasped. "They're really angry, aren't they?"

Ricki started chewing on a thumbnail. "It's awful."

"I don't mean to pick on you, Annie," said Andy. "I'm sorry about that 'A-Neata' business. It's just that . . . I thought it was a friendly way of pointing out a problem."

"What problem?"

"Well . . ." Andy hesitated. "Um, your . . . untidy habits."

"Untidy habits?"

Andy nodded. "Things are getting to be a real mess."

"Andy, it doesn't seem to worry you that your friends march in and out of this house at all hours, slapping clay on the dining room table or spraying sawdust all over the den. Yet if I leave my hairpins in the bathtub, it's a real mess to you. That's no way to live. I feel as if I'm walking on eggshells trying to stay neat to your satisfaction."

"Could have fooled me," Andy said.

Anita shot him a sharp sideways look.

"Oh, Ricki," Vanessa whispered. "We've got to—"

"I know. Do something."

Together, the girls walked out from behind the door toward their parents.

Ricki cleared her throat.

Vanessa began. "Dad, I—"

Anita didn't hear her. "Look, Andy. That sarcastic attitude of yours is exactly what I'm talking about. It's infuriating."

"How do you think I feel, Annie, when I clear off our dresser top and half an hour later come in to find it covered with computer printout?"

"How do you think *I* feel," Anita replied, "when I fold a load of bath towels crosswise and you come and refold them lengthwise?"

They didn't seem to notice Vanessa and Ricki standing between them. The girls were right under their parents' noses, and still the argument steamed on.

"Mom," Ricki tried. "Listen, we think—"

"Of course I'm going to refold the towels," Andy interrupted. "You fold them crookedly."

Anita rolled her eyes. So did Ricki. Then Ricki put one finger in each corner of her mouth and whistled as loud as she could.

The grown-ups went quiet. They looked at Ricki, then at Vanessa.

"Please," said Vanessa, "listen to us."

"We think you should stop arguing," Ricki said.

"Yes," Vanessa continued. "Messiness isn't that important."

"Neatness isn't, either," added Ricki.

"Neat people and messy people," said Vanessa, "should be able to get along."

"Yeah. No matter how neat the neat people want things to be."

"And no matter how messed up the messy people make things."

"Things never get *that* messy, anyway," said Ricki.

"Well, even if they do," Vanessa said, "neat people should be patient."

Ricki nodded. "Right, even if the neat people drive the rest of us up the wall, we should be able to stay calm."

"Yes," agreed Vanessa, "even if things get so messy that you can't cross the room anymore—"

"Or even if you start feeling like you live in a hotel instead of in a house," said Ricki.

"Or even if you feel like you're living in a pigsty," said Vanessa.

"Girls," said Andy.

"Or in a hospital," Ricki went on.

"Girls!" insisted Anita.

Vanessa's cheeks were red as tomatoes, and her chin jutted out fiercely.

Ricki grabbed a deep breath, then let it out in a snort. She crossed her arms.

"I think," said Andy, "we all need to sit down and have a talk."

Anita nodded. "Definitely. A long one."

Ricki's arms stayed crossed. Vanessa's chin jutted out farther. They glared at each other.

A waiter wearing rainbow-striped suspenders brought four frozen yogurt shakes and four Happily Healthful sandwiches.

Vanessa reached for her shake, strawberry flavored, and took a long, deep swallow through the straw.

Ricki bit a huge chunk out of her turkey sandwich. It was one of the few items on the Happy Carrot menu that contained no nuts or seeds.

"Well, this ought to help us all feel a little better," said her mother, sipping on her vanilla shake.

Andy nodded. "I think part of today's problem was that we skipped lunch." He bit into his avocado on rye.

"Yes, part of it," agreed Anita. "But not all of it."

Andy nodded again. "We've also skipped important talks we should have been having these past few weeks."

"Do we have to talk now?" Ricki asked between mouthfuls.

"Well, that was the idea," her mother answered.

Vanessa's stomach felt upside down. "Can't we wait?" The last thing she wanted at that moment was more arguing.

Silently, Ricki agreed. She'd had enough of the Sisters War for one day.

Andy grinned softly at them. "Hey, you two act like we're about to boil in oil. It's not that grim."

"I'm sick of arguments," Ricki said.

Her mother slipped an arm around her. "Hon, so are we."

"Then why do you have so many of them?" Vanessa asked.

"Hmm," Andy said. "Isn't this is a case of the pot calling the kettle black?"

"The who doing the what?" Ricki scrunched up her nose.

"It's an expression," Anita explained, "from the days when pots and kettles were both black. The point is, Andy and I have disagreements, just like you and Vanessa do, don't you?"

Vanessa looked up from her shake. She and Ricki both shrugged.

"Arguing is completely natural for people who live together," said Andy. "Happens all the time."

"If it didn't happen, it would probably mean we weren't expressing our feelings about problems that come up," Anita added.

"We probably are going to hit a few snags," Andy went on, "considering the fact that our family is composed of four wonderful, fascinating, and very different personalities."

"And, you know," said Anita, "officially, we are what is known as a 'blended' family. Single parents, each with their own kids getting together. Andy and I have been reading some information about it."

"According to the Stepfamily Association of America," Andy said, "one-fifth of all kids under eighteen in the United States is a member of a blended family or stepfamily."

"Really?" Vanessa asked. "One-fifth? That's one out of every five kids."

Anita nodded. "Hundreds of new blended families form each day. There are a lot of us."

"And we each have our own special joys and problems," added Andy.

"For instance," said Anita, "one of *our* family's special problems right now seems to be that we're sometimes too good at expressing our feelings. Other times we're not good enough."

"So, we've been thinking, maybe we should set aside a time every week for talks like this one," Andy said.

"You mean, appointments?" Vanessa raised an eyebrow.

"Like business meetings?" asked Ricki.

Anita laughed. "Well, maybe not that formal."

"More like family meetings," said Andy. "A special time for working on problems."

"With the idea being to talk about a problem *before* it upsets you enough to argue about it," Anita said.

"Oh," said Vanessa. "Like the summit meetings that different countries' leaders have to avoid wars."

"Or powwows that Native Americans had," added Ricki.

"Well, something like that," said Anita.

Andy chuckled. "Right. Family powwows to avoid wars. I like that."

Vanessa leaned her head to the side. "You mean, if something's bothering me, I bring it up at the powwow instead of waiting until it gets to the point of making me really angry."

"Exactly." Anita nodded.

"What if whatever's bugging me makes me mad right away?" Ricki asked. "I mean, what if I don't have time to wait until the powwow?"

Andy shrugged. "Well, we're still going to have arguments sometimes. But at the powwows, we won't be acting in the heat of the moment. We can be more calm and considerate of one another's feelings. We can think about things before we say them, so that we don't say things we don't mean."

"I'm sure we each have concerns at this very moment," said Anita. "Things we're already upset about and haven't resolved with one another yet."

"You can say that again." Ricki bunched her mouth sideways.

Andy laughed. "Does that mean you're volunteering? Should we go ahead and have Powwow Number One now?"

Ricki glanced at Vanessa, who peeked back at her.

"That sounds good to me," offered Anita. "I think we do have a few things to clear up from earlier this afternoon."

Ricki squirmed. She felt as if she stood on the edge of an icy pool of water, about to dive in.

"I, uh," she began. "Well, I'm kind of tired of having to worry about being neat all the time."

Vanessa nodded. "I'm tired of things being messy."

Andy and Anita gave each other looks.

"Those," said Anita with a smile, "seem to be very common problems in our family."

"Should I, uh, go on and complain about more stuff?" asked Ricki.

"Sure." Andy nodded. "Please."

"Well, I kind of . . ." She swallowed. "Sometimes I feel that our house, well, that it's not really *my* house, too. I mean, that I don't really have a say in things. Like, our room. And, well, all the visitors and things.

123

The artists and music people. Sometimes I feel kind of uncomfortable around them. Like, the other morning I woke up and went into our bathroom in the hall, and Zinna the painter was in there mixing up some kind of orange gooky paint in the sink.''

Andy gave her an embarrassed look and nodded. "I can see how that would be disconcerting.''

"Definitely," agreed Anita. She frowned at Andy and tapped a fingernail on the tabletop. "I enjoy your friends, hon. But sometimes they can be a bit much.''

"Well," Andy began, "after we remodel the attic, I'll start on converting the garage into music and art studios. But meanwhile, how about if I have my pals show up only at certain hours, agreed to in advance at our powwows?''

Ricki and her mother nodded.

"What about the neatness problem?" asked Vanessa. "How do we solve that?''

"I think that one might be a little thornier," said Anita. "But I have an idea. First, it seems we could all be a little more flexible.''

"Yeah," Ricki said, eyeing Vanessa. "Like not throwing a fit if things aren't perfect.''

Her mother sighed. "You and I have to be more flexible, too, Ricki. For instance, we have to recognize that our housework habits are, well, unusually . . . relaxed, shall we say? It won't kill us to shape up a bit and sit down with the rest of the family to establish a regular system for chores. Would that help, Vanessa?''

"I think so," Vanessa agreed. "I think the main thing that bothers me is when you and Ricki sort of make fun of Dad and me about being neat. And roll your eyes and things when we say we think something needs to be cleaned or whatever.''

Anita smiled sheepishly at Ricki. ''I guess we have been doing such things, haven't we?''

Ricki bunched her mouth to the side. She had to admit it was true. No one was innocent in the family arguments. They had all shown their worst behavior at one time or another. Now, it seemed they were all getting a chance to straighten out.

Vanessa suddenly felt lighter. She looked around the table at her father, Anita, Ricki, and realized something. They truly were a family, with family spats just like any other. They had problems, but they could solve them.

''Anita and I have another idea,'' added Andy. ''Neither of you is going to like it, though. We've come to a decision, and we're going to insist that you at least give it a try.''

Vanessa's light feeling started to fizzle.

Ricki took a deep breath to get ready.

Before their parents said another word, both girls knew what the bright idea would be.

Chapter Thirteen

Separate rooms.

The very thought of it made Vanessa feel cold. She would be alone again. No Ricki to whisper and giggle with at all hours. So what if Ricki was, well, a little untidy? And had awful taste in posters. If they gave up on rooming together now, it would mean admitting failure! Practically a defeat of the Sisters Scheme!

Ricki couldn't imagine a room without Vanessa. Even though Vee could be awfully picky. And even though sharing had caused a lot of arguments, like Andy and Anita said. Still, she and Vanessa had a lot of fun times sharing their room. And the whole point of being sisters was to be together, not a whole room apart, like in a hotel!

Anita and Andy wouldn't listen to reason. They had made up their minds, together. And once they did that, they were about as moveable as the Rock of Gibraltar.

Vanessa stood in the hall outside the door of the guest room, now Ricki's room, reading the signs.

ENTER AT YOUR OWN RISK
NO BOZOS
DANGER: FALLING ROCKS
GENIUS AT WORK
BEWARE OF BALONEY

There were dozens of them. Some of the signs were tin metal plates Ricki had gotten at the flea market they'd gone to with Suzanne and Gordon. Others were bumper stickers she'd been collecting.

Vanessa thought it looked tacky to have all that pinned on the door. But of course, it was none of her business. At Family Powwow Number Three that week, they had all decided that you got to do more or less whatever you wanted to and in your own room. No matter how tacky.

Vanessa knocked.

"Yeah?" Ricki called.

Vanessa opened the door and was hit by a blast of the music she'd heard faintly in the hall. She tried to smile.

This was not the kind of visit she'd had in mind. The reason she'd come to Ricki's room was that it was already the middle of August, and Mama still hadn't called. She felt anxious.

"Hi," Vanessa yelled above the music.

"Hi," Ricki yelled back. She was lying on her stomach on her bed, feet up in the air behind her. They waved back and forth in time to the fast beat.

"What are you listening to?" Vanessa yelled.

"Dweezil Zappa. Different, huh? Like it?"

Vanessa tried another smile. "Uh, it's, uh, interesting." She sat down in Ricki's desk chair, which appeared to be the one piece of furniture not hidden under clothes, camera equipment, and Rock Beat magazines. "Could you turn it down a little?"

Ricki shrugged and rolled over to her cassette player on the nightstand. "Sure."

Vanessa took a deep breath. She could hear again.

"Andy helped me find this tape at the record shop at the mall," said Ricki, snapping her fingers to the beat. "Spent my week's allowance, but it was worth it."

"Oh," said Vanessa. It had been two weeks since Andy and Anita had helped Ricki move her stuff to the spare room. There were a few advantages, Vanessa decided. For example, Ricki seemed to believe that if a piece of music was good, it was better louder. And to top it off, she had gotten interested in some very weird music since Andy started giving her guitar lessons. Vanessa didn't think she could handle listening to it all day long.

"Well, Vee, how are you doing?" Ricki asked, still swinging her feet.

"Oh, fine, thanks. Just fine."

Ricki hated this part of having separate rooms. The politeness. In each other's territories, she and Vanessa acted like strangers instead of sisters. She sighed. "You know, Vee, I miss you."

"Oh, Ricki, I've been missing you, too," Vanessa admitted. "It's so odd. Almost as if we're in different countries instead of just different rooms."

Ricki nodded. "Even though we visit all the time."

"And watch 'Day After Day' together."

"And have breakfast and lunch and dinner together."

"It's just not the same." Vanessa sighed.

"But," began Ricki hesitantly, "it's not as bad as we thought it would be, is it?" She didn't want to admit what a relief it was not to have to look at the frilly little girl stuff in Vanessa's room anymore or to worry about leaving a towel on the floor or a hairbrush on the desk.

"No, it's not as bad," Vanessa agreed. "We are still sisters."

Ricki smiled. "You bet. And best buddies."

"Absolutely! Scoot over." Vanessa sat next to Ricki cross-legged. "Even if you do have terrible taste in music."

"I do? What about you and those weird things you've been practicing?"

Vanessa raised an eyebrow. "My music is classical. Those 'weird things' happen to be by a composer named Eric Satie."

Ricki shrugged. "Call it what you want. It still sounds weird."

Vanessa shrugged back. "Your opinion."

"Vee." Ricki rolled over on her back to look up at her friend. "You know what?"

"What?"

"You and I can have arguments these days without having, well, arguments."

Vanessa laughed. "I know. We still argue, but . . ."

"It's kind of more quiet. Maybe because of the pow-wows. I think they've helped a lot more than separate rooms have. And I don't think we're, like, total dweebs or anything because we had to have separate rooms."

"I don't either. In fact, I think we're champs. It's not all pairs of best friends who figure out how to become sisters!"

129

"Right!" agreed Ricki, holding out her hand for a high five.

"You know," said Vanessa after they slapped their palms together, "even Dad and Anita are arguing less since we've been having the powwows, and *they* don't have separate rooms."

Ricki nodded. "Yeah. They are fighting less, aren't they? Or maybe they just don't fight in front of us so much."

"Hmm. That's possible. I guess they figured out that it worries us."

"And maybe they got sick of us butting in." Ricki rolled back over on her stomach.

Vanessa nodded. "I've been thinking about that. How we used to try to stop their arguments. It never really worked, did it? The arguments were just postponed, not cancelled, whenever we got involved."

"They're probably always going to argue, aren't they?" Ricki sighed. "Your dad and my mom are so different."

"He's mellow," said Vanessa. "She's high-strung."

"His friends are artists and musicians. Hers are bankers and lawyers." Ricki tapped a finger on her chin.

"She's tall. He's short," Vanessa added.

"Hey, that one doesn't count, remember? We decided that when we came up with the Scheme."

"We also decided," said Vanessa, "that opposites attract. That is, if they're not *too* opposite."

"Right," agreed Ricki. "Kind of like two pieces of a puzzle fitting together. They may be shaped really differently, but they belong together."

Vanessa smiled. "It's funny. "You and I will probably always fight sometimes, because we're so different.

130

But at the same time, that's why we're such good friends. *Because* we're different.''

"We make a good team." Ricki grinned. "Like on a softball team, where you need players with different skills. Good hitters, good pitchers, good runners . . .''

"I wish we would never, ever have another argument, Ricki!''

Ricki shook her head. "Dream on.''

"I guess it's kind of hard work being sisters.'' Vanessa sighed.

"Yeah." Ricki nodded. "It's even harder being a family!''

"Complicated, isn't it?" Vanessa asked.

"Juggling everybody's feelings and stuff to keep them happy," Ricki went on.

Vanessa leaned her head to the side. "Maybe . . . maybe we try too hard. I mean, maybe we should just relax.''

"Like, not butt in on Mom's and Andy's fights?" suggested Ricki.

Vanessa nodded. "Concentrate on just being sisters, first of all. Let Dad and Anita worry about being married.''

"Even though it was our idea that they *get* married?''

"Well, nobody dragged them to the altar." Vanessa smiled.

Ricki giggled. "They did seem pretty willing." She stuck out her hand. "Let's shake on it, Vee. No more butting in, okay?''

Vanessa shook hands enthusiastically. "Cross our hearts.''

With their fingers, they both drew little X's over their chests.

There was a knock on the door.

"Anybody home?" Andy called from the hall.

"Come in," yelled Ricki.

He opened the door. "Here you are. The two peas. In a pod, as usual."

Vanessa and Ricki giggled.

"Hey, is this the Dweezil Zappa tape?" Andy asked.

"Yeah. This song is called 'Can't Ruin Me.' " Ricki handed him the cassette box.

"Oh, look at this," said Andy. "Dweezil's dad, Frank, co-produced the album."

"Frank who?" Ricki asked. "I know Dweezil's sister, Moon, does vocals."

Andy shook his head and grinned. "Hey, Frank Zappa, of course. A legend in his own time."

Listening to Andy and Ricki talk, Vanessa frowned. "I've never heard of any of these people."

Ricki laughed. "Well, *I've* never heard of all the music and art stuff *you* talk about."

"I've got something completely new to talk about," Andy interrupted. "And it's a good thing you're both sitting down before I tell you."

"Huh? Why?" Ricki asked.

Andy cleared his throat. "Well, I—"

"Oh, Dad!" Vanessa clapped her hands "Is it— Are you— Are we going to have a little brother or sister?"

Ricki sat up straight. "A little brother or sister? Are we? Wow, I never even thought about—"

"Girls." Andy grinned. "Let's not get carried away. No, we are not having a little brother or sister." Then he laughed. "Although I wouldn't be surprised if you two decided to make that your next plan."

"Then what is it?" asked Vanessa.

"Remember I promised to get some information about this house? Its former owners?" Andy began. "Well, I finally got in touch with my former guitar student, Pierre, the one who sold the house to me. Now, I want you to take this with a grain of salt, okay? It's only rumor, and I don't want you to get carried away with it—"

"With what?" Ricki was so excited she could barely sit still.

Andy cleared his throat. "I've debated on whether or not to tell you. You have to promise me you won't exaggerate its importance."

"We promise, Dad, absolutely!" Vanessa vowed.

With a sigh, Andy said, "Okay. Pierre says one of the reasons he sold me this house so cheaply was that, well, as he puts it, there were 'unexplained phenomena' here."

"Huh?" Ricki squinted. "What's that?"

"More or less," Andy said, "it means weird events that no one can figure out."

Vanessa's eyebrows shot upward. "You mean—you mean—"

"Now, Vee. You promised," Andy warned, wagging a finger at her.

"But 'unexplained phenomena,' " Vanessa went on, "equals Emmett!"

"Hey!" Ricki's eyes widened. "You mean other people have heard him, too?"

"Girls, what I'm saying is that several people who lived here before us heard weird noises. I'm *not* saying anyone heard Emmett."

Ricki and Vanessa looked at each other gleefully.

133

"Hah! See, Dad? See?" Vanessa cried. "We're not the only ones! Other people—"

Andy cut in. "Other people heard noises, Vee. Period. They got spooked and moved out. This happened about every six months, Pierre says, so he kept having to find new people to rent the place, and when he got tired of that, well, I jumped in." Andy grinned.

"Then you don't believe our house is haunted?" Ricki asked.

Andy shook his head. "Of course not. But I do believe something has been making those noises you've heard, and I intend to find out what."

"Did Pierre say anything about Clementine Hewitt?" Ricki asked.

"All he knows is that the Hewitt family were the first ones to live here. They had the house built for them in 1924. They moved out in 1938."

"But Pierre doesn't know where they went?" Vanessa asked.

Andy shook his head. "Sorry. But he said we should ask some of the neighbors around here. Meanwhile, my peas, I've got a student coming in five minutes, so I'd better go downstairs. But remember, don't blow all this out of proportion, okay?"

On his way out, he gave them a look that was half-grin, half-warning.

The minute he shut the door behind him, Ricki flew off the bed and started jumping up and down. "Hooray! We have a haunted house! This is cool!"

Vanessa giggled. "But it still gives me the shivers."

"Me, too," Ricki agreed. "Not as bad as it used to, though. Vee, when can we read the letters? Aunt Allegra said—"

"I know what Aunt Allegra said, Ricki. You sound like a broken record. It still seems wrong—"

"Oh, for Pete's sake." Ricki rolled her eyes. "Clementine, wherever she is, probably doesn't even *remember* those letters, much less care if we read them."

"Well, I suppose if there is an Emmett," said Vanessa, "it would make him feel more at home, like Aunt Allegra said, to hear the letters read aloud."

Ricki grinned ear to ear. "So we can read 'em now?"

Vanessa raised an eyebrow. "I'll think about it."

Ricki rolled her eyes.

That evening after dinner, Ricki knocked on Vanessa's door. The sounds of Vanessa practicing cello had stopped just a few minutes before. Now there was no answer.

"Vee, you in there?" Ricki opened the door. She saw the cello but not Vanessa.

"Wait, I didn't say come in!" a voice protested.

The voice came from the closet, where Vanessa sat with a small wooden box in her lap and a stack of yellowed envelopes in her hands.

Even from across the room, Ricki could see Vanessa's deep red blush.

"Hmm." Ricki crossed her arms. "I see. You're busy, aren't you?"

"I was not reading the letters, if that's what you're implying." Vanessa pursed her lips.

"Right," Ricki replied. "And the moon is blue."

"Stop being sarcastic. I swear I was not reading the letters, all right?"

Ricki recrossed her arms. "But you were thinking about it, weren't you?"

135

Vanessa nodded.

"Hey, great!" Ricki strode across the room and plopped down next to her friend.

While Ricki fidgeted there, Vanessa slowly thumbed through the envelopes. At the sight of the last one, Ricki stopped fidgeting.

"Hey, look at that," she said.

"What?" asked Vanessa.

"The last one's addressed *to* Mr. Emmett Tibbs, Senior, from Clementine. Maybe she's telling him to go fly a kite."

"Hmm." Vanessa nodded. "But 'Senior'? Sounds like she was writing to Emmett's father. Anyway, this letter was never mailed. There's no postmark. The return address is Miss Clementine Hewitt, 244 Mariposa Lane, Berkeley, Calif—"

"244?" Ricki grabbed the envelope. "Let me see that."

"That's not our address," said Vanessa. "This house is at 202. Clementine made a mistake. 244 would be all the way down the street, wouldn't it?"

"Yeah, it would," agreed Ricki. "Isn't that weird, to write your own address wrong?"

Vanessa nodded. "All the letters from Emmett are to 202 Mariposa, our address."

"Maybe *he* had it wrong," Ricki suggested.

"No. Dad's friend Pierre says this was the Hewitt's home."

"Oh, that's right. Well, you know there is one way to solve this mystery." Ricki grinned hopefully.

"Well." Vanessa shrugged a shoulder. "I guess it wouldn't be bad to read just this one letter."

Ricki watched eagerly as Vanessa's index finger skimmed the envelope's open edge.

Then they both heard Andy's footsteps on the stairs. "Vee," he called. "Phone for you!"

Ricki bunched her mouth to the side. Shucks! They had come so close!

Vanessa's thoughts were very different. Mama, finally calling!

People born on August 17 were Leos, according to the newspaper astrology column, and Leos were supposed to be loyal, bossy, and sulk a lot.

Vanessa, lying in the hammock on the back deck, frowned at the newspaper. She was loyal, that much was true. But bossy? Sulky? Never!

The astrologer also predicted that Leos with birthdays on August 17 were supposed to have an exciting, informative one that year.

Vanessa folded the newspaper and dropped it on the picnic table. Today was August 17, her birthday, and it was anything but surprising or informative. So far it had been just like any other day. Except for one thing. She hardly ever got so confused.

On the one hand, she felt sad. Mama's phone call Wednesday night had been to say that she couldn't visit at all in August and instead would come around the Christmas holidays. During their talk, Vanessa had to bite both cheeks to keep from sniffling.

On the other hand, she felt deep relief. And that made her feel guilty. You weren't supposed to feel relieved about your own mother not coming to see you, were you?

137

Vanessa decided she had absolutely never, ever felt so confused. Or so lonely.

She wandered into the kitchen and with a sponge wiped up a few stray breakfast crumbs. Andy was working on a new composition in the living room. Hours ago, Ricki and Anita had gone to Uncle Mario's to pick up Vanessa's birthday cake for the big family party they were planning for her that afternoon. Vanessa knew the party would be a lot of fun, but in the meantime, she wished she had company. Maybe Nona and Papa would call soon.

Just as she was thinking about calling them herself, she heard an odd noise off in the distance. It sounded like a dog barking several blocks away.

She picked up the kitchen phone and started dialing her grandparents' number. The barking got louder. By the time she punched in the last digit, Vanessa heard the sputtery sound of Anita's small car pulling into the driveway.

And then there was a bark. A big, loud bark.

Slowly, Vanessa put the phone back in its cradle.

Maybe it was her imagination. Lots of dogs had big, loud barks. Not just one particular, special dog. Anyway, what would that one special dog be doing in Anita's car?

Holding her breath, Vanessa closed her eyes. Was it fair to make a birthday wish *before* you got your cake?

Chapter Fourteen

The first thing Vanessa saw when she opened the front door was fur. A lot of it. All black.

"Yuck! Mom, look! He's licking Vee's nose!" Ricki cried.

Vanessa didn't hear. All she knew was that two gigantic paws rested on her shoulders, two brown eyes looked lovingly at her from under long, shaggy eyebrows, and a huge pink tongue was giving her whole face a thorough bath.

"I think she'll survive," Anita told Ricki, smiling.

For a moment, Ricki wondered if Kirby would ever let go of her friend, or vice versa. Vanessa's arms were wrapped so tightly around the dog that he probably couldn't have left her alone even if he'd wanted to, which, apparently, he hadn't the least bit of interest in doing.

"If that isn't a case of true love," said Andy from the living room window, "I don't know what is." He gazed out at his daughter on the porch.

"What—? How—?" Vanessa began, but couldn't make it through a whole question. For one thing, Kirby was still slurping her face, and for another, she was still too shocked.

"Happy birthday," said Ricki. Having the big beast around wasn't exactly *her* idea of fun, but it sure seemed to make Vanessa happy.

"Birthday?" Vanessa sputtered.

Kirby finally dropped his paws to the porch floor, then went to work washing Vanessa's hands.

"Yes, sweetie, happy birthday." Anita climbed the porch stairs and put an arm around Vanessa. "I think that's what Kirby's trying to say. Along with, he's *very* happy to see you."

"But— But I thought— Your allergies—?"

Anita nodded. "Are you ready for a long story?"

She guided Vanessa to the porch chairs. Andy and Ricki joined them. After a few minutes, Vanessa thought she finally had the whole thing straight.

"You mean you've been visiting Kirby this month?" she asked Anita, while stroking the wavy fur on Kirby's back. He lay at her feet, taking a contented snooze after all the excitement.

"My doctor," said Anita, "told me it was possible I had grown out of my childhood allergies. After all, I hadn't really been around dogs since I was very young. So I called Shelley Kahn, Kirby's foster guardian, and she said she'd be delighted to let me visit her house and see what happened."

"And that's how Anita lost her heart," Andy told the girls. "I knew it the first day she went over there. She came home with this moony look in her eyes."

Anita smiled sheepishly. "Well, he *is* awfully hard to resist. Aren't you, fella?" She reached down and scratched behind Kirby's ears.

"You're not allergic to him anymore?" asked Vanessa. "Really? Are you sure?"

140

"The doctor says I'm clear. I've spent a lot of time with Kirby this month, along with Shelley's six other dogs, and had not a bit of a reaction. The doctor says it will help that our house has hardwood floors instead of carpeting. We can vacuum more thoroughly to prevent fur build-up. And, according to Kirby's vet, he is apparently some kind of part poodle mix. They don't shed much."

"Poodle?" Ricki repeated, eyes wide. *"That* is a poodle?"

"From what I understand," said Andy, "poodles do come in jumbo sizes."

"He's got other breeds mixed in, too," Anita went on. "I think he looks just like an Irish wolfhound. They're enormous."

"Does that mean he's going to grow?" asked Ricki, frowning.

Anita laughed. "Well, hon, you heard what the vet said this morning. Kirby's just a puppy. Probably only a year old."

Ricki sighed. "I guess we won't have to worry much about burglars."

Vanessa felt she might explode with happiness. Just an hour ago she had been sad and confused. Not to mention lonely. But now, with Kirby *and* her family around, who could be lonely?

"I think," she said, giving Anita a hug, "this is the best birthday I've ever had!"

On the backyard patio that afternoon, Ricki sipped pineapple punch from a paper cup. She stood next to Andy, who was talking to a round, bald man with black-rimmed glasses and a pipe.

He was their neighbor, Dr. Rosen, from the dark, ivy-covered house next door that looked like the castle in *Madness of the Dark*. Dr. Rosen had just told Andy that he was a retired professor.

Ricki swallowed the punch in a gulp.

Andy had spotted Dr. Rosen over in his backyard a few minutes before and had invited him to Vanessa's birthday party. It would have been rude not to, Ricki supposed, since he was their neighbor and they had music and food and balloons and a whole patio full of guests. But Ricki couldn't help wondering if Dr. Rosen ran an experiment laboratory in his basement.

She glanced around for Vanessa, who, of course, was under the trees playing fetch with Kirby, Aunt Laura, and the little cousins. Gordon, Suzanne, Mrs. Quan, and the other guests watched from the patio.

"Yes. I grew up," Dr. Rosen was saying between long drags on his pipe, "in my house. My father . . . bought it . . . in . . ."

Ricki watched him, frowning. For one thing, she couldn't stand smoke. For another, waiting for him to finish sentences was like waiting for water to boil. She had never heard anyone talk so slowly. How did he manage not to fall asleep between words? She wondered if a person could pass out from calmness.

Then it hit her. "Did—did you say you grew up there?" she asked quietly.

Dr. Rosen looked down at her as if noticing her for the first time. Slowly, he nodded. Smoke from his pipe swirled around his eyes.

Ricki excused herself and ran to get Vanessa. Dr. Rosen must know about Clementine Hewitt. Maybe, finally, Vanessa would agree to read the letters.

By the time Ricki managed to drag Vanessa away from the fetch game, Andy had led Dr. Rosen inside for a tour of the remodeling.

The girls and Kirby caught up with them in the upstairs hall.

"The Hewitts," Dr. Rosen was saying to Andy. "Oh, yes. I certainly do know about them." Having left his pipe outside, he was talking a little faster than before.

Ricki poked Vanessa in the ribs and whispered, "See?"

Still panting from the mad dash upstairs, Vanessa asked, "What do you know about them, Dr. Rosen?"

Again, he looked down as if the girls hadn't existed before.

"The Hewitts—" he began.

"Wait, did you just hear something?" Andy asked.

"Well, yes." Dr. Hewitt nodded. "A distinct sound, exactly like—"

"Snoring!" cried Vanessa.

"I heard it, too!" Ricki joined in.

Andy frowned. "Just a second ago I thought I—"

He was interrupted by a low, grumbly rumble from above.

"Dad, it's—it's—" Vanessa swallowed.

"Emmett!" Ricki finished for her.

Dr. Rosen gave the girls an odd look over his glasses. "Emmett?"

Then, suddenly, something black flew past them up the attic stairs. From the ceiling above came a flurry of paw thuds and barking.

"Kirby!" Vanessa called, running upstairs after him. "Oh, no! See? Dogs know about ghosts!"

Right behind her, Andy said, "I knew it had to be something in the attic!"

Ricki and Dr. Rosen followed, and soon they heard Anita on the stairs, too. "What's going on? What's all the commotion?" she demanded.

"Kirby's chasing Emmett!" Ricki explained, leaning down into the stairwell.

"Who's Emmett?" Uncle Mario was behind Anita, along with Aunt Ruth and the kids.

"What is wrong? Oof!" Mrs. Quan cried. "Ah, these stairs are too steep for me."

"I'll give you an arm," Gordon offered.

"Up we go." Suzanne supported her on the other side.

In moments the whole birthday gathering stood in the attic.

"I see no Emmett," Mrs. Quan said, puffing.

"Who's Emmett?" asked Uncle Mario.

"Where's Kirby?" cried Vanessa.

He had vanished. The only trace of him was the muffled sound of barking, and that was coming from behind the wall!

Vanessa's heart pounded in worry. Where could Kirby be?

"Hmm." Dr. Rosen nodded. "Very interesting. It appears the dog has found his way into the crawl space of your attic."

Andy grabbed a flashlight off a crate. Slowly, he walked with it along the wall. "But how? I never noticed—" He stopped behind an old chest of drawers, where the flashlight beam was suddenly swallowed by a low, dark hole in the wall.

"Well, I'll be," he whispered.

Ricki gasped. "A secret passage!"

"Nothing of the kind," Dr. Rosen objected. "Just crawl space for maintenance. Many older homes have them."

Vanessa ran to the little doorway. "Kirby! Come out of there!"

The barking went on.

Andy shone the light in to reveal a big furry rump and busily wagging tail.

"Kirby!" Vanessa called.

A loud screech pierced the air.

Ricki's eyes went wide. "He's cornered Emmett!"

Uncle Mario threw his hands up in the air. "Who the heck is Emmett?"

Aunt Laura shook her head. "That's no Emmett." She grinned. "Not at all. But I do think you'd better get Kirby out of there. He could get hurt. Or he could break up a family."

"What?" Anita frowned. "Which family?"

"I agree," said Dr. Rosen. "That screeching sound belongs to one type of being. I've had a few in my house, as well."

"A being?" Ricki's eyes went wider. Her head filled with images of the spaghetti-head monsters overflowing from Dr. Rosen's house into theirs.

Vanessa continued calling to Kirby. "Kirby, please! Come out *now!*"

Finally, his rump started moving in reverse. Inch by inch he backed out of the narrow passage, still barking. Vanessa grabbed onto his collar, just in case he decided on another exploration.

"I believe," began Dr. Rosen," the Latin name of the creature is *arakunem,* is it not?"

Aunt Laura nodded. "It means 'hand-scratcher.' "

"Hold on," Gordon said, grinning. "I think I'm beginning to get it. Laura, you're a biologist, right? And *arakunem*. That sounds like . . ."

Mrs. Quan jumped in. "Raccoon. Is it not so? I know these animals. Like little bears."

"Wait," said Aunt Ruth. "If you're saying that Kirby was after raccoons in that passage—"

"Probably a whole family of them," said Aunt Laura. "The screeching sounds come from young ones in distress."

"Then *who*," asked Uncle Mario in complete exasperation, "is Emmett?"

Andy laughed. "Emmett, my friends, has turned out to be a family of raccoons."

"Have you been hearing odd noises?" asked Dr. Rosen. "Particularly at night? Previous occupants here complained of it. I tried to explain to them that it was only the little mammals, but . . ." He shrugged.

"Raccoons are nocturnal," said Aunt Laura. "Very active and playful. Not to mention vocal."

"Because of the way these older homes were designed," added Dr. Rosen, "you have a kind of built-in audio system in the crawl space and heating ducts. Sound travels to other parts of the house, sometimes in an echoing, distorted fashion."

"But Vee and I were the only ones who ever heard the noises," said Ricki, "and they always sounded like they were in the hall."

Andy nodded. "That makes sense. There's a big air exchange vent in the hall, along the wall close to your rooms. It might act like a giant speaker."

"Meanwhile," said Anita, "those poor creatures must

146

be terrified. We can't leave them in there, can we? For one thing, Kirby will probably go in again."

"And if you're remodeling the attic," added Aunt Laura, "you probably won't want them going in and out the window on their night forays for food."

"You might call Ms. Hewitt," said Dr. Rosen.

Both Ricki's and Vanessa's heads whirled to face him.

"Ms. who?" asked Vanessa slowly.

"Our neighbor, Ms. Hewitt. At the end of the street. Her house is hard to see. Number 244 Mariposa. She runs a wild animal hospice there."

Vanessa's brain reeled. Hewitt? Number 244?

Ricki kept thinking of a lion's head. A lion's head? Why would *that* pop into her head? she wondered. Then, suddenly, she remembered. C.H.! The initials on the brass lion's head door knocker at the scary house down the street.

"Ricki!" Vanessa whispered.

Almost at the same moment, Ricki whispered, "Vanessa!"

Dr. Rosen was saying, "As a matter of fact, Ms. Hewitt was one of the original residents of this house. She would have stayed here, most likely, if it hadn't been for the *arakunem*. A beau of hers, Emmett Tibbs—"

"Emmett?" repeated Uncle Mario.

"Yes." Dr. Rosen trained his owlish gaze on Uncle Mario. "Emmett Tibbs drowned at sea."

Ricki sucked in a breath. "He did?"

After a glance down at her, Dr. Rosen stared off above her head, deep in thought. "Tibbs's mishap occurred soon after Clementine became engaged to another young man, and the rumor spread that his spirit had come to haunt her family's house.''

"How sad.'' Aunt Ruth sighed.

"The Hewitts,'' continued Dr. Rosen, "plagued by the disturbing noises, no doubt caused by ancestors of the creatures you yourselves have heard, sold this house and moved down the street. Ms. Hewitt remains there.''

"Poor Emmett,'' said Anita, shaking her head.

"Poor *arakunem*,'' said Andy. "We have to evict them.''

"Ms. Hewitt accepts injured and displaced wild animals from all over the county,'' said Dr. Rosen. "A local animal protection organization delivers supplies to her. She heals and prepares the animals for the wild. A word of caution, though, about contacting her. She's a bit of a loner. Doesn't often venture beyond her home. Approach her with extreme courtesy.''

"Hmm. Sounds like a job for our two ghostbusters here, doesn't it?'' Andy grinned at the girls. "The Sister Sleuths.''

Vanessa blushed fiercely. Ricki bunched her mouth sideways. They both wished Andy would spare them the humor.

Meanwhile, they were still trying to recover from the afternoon's surprises. Emmett was a bunch of raccoons? Clementine Hewitt lived down the street?

Ricki sighed. Now Vanessa would probably never let them read the letters. Plus, they'd have to go back to that spooky house.

Vanessa chewed on her cheek. Could Clementine be that scary-looking person with the wild white hair? She couldn't imagine talking to her. *And* handing over the letters.

148

Oh well, Ricki decided. It could be worse. Emmett could have turned out to be a family of skunks!

"Something," said Mrs. Quan, breaking into the girls' thoughts, "has been forgotten." Her wide, brown-skinned face looked cloudy.

Everyone went quiet.

Then Mrs. Quan burst into a bright smile. "The party!"

Laughing, they all followed her back to the patio. There, Vanessa blew out the candles on her big strawberry cream cake. For that year, she had already made her wish and gotten it—Kirby! She thought about how amazing the day had been. "Surprising and informative," after all.

After cutting slices of cake for all her guests, Vanessa finally cut a piece for herself. She was just about to take a bite of it when she heard slurping sounds. She froze. The sounds came from under the table. Had a new family of raccoons settled there? She held her breath. If Kirby were to hear them, there would be mayhem!

Vanessa leaned over and lifted up the tablecloth.

Two large brown eyes gazed shyly back at her.

"Kirby! What are you—!"

Then she saw Ricki, on the other side, under the table, holding an empty plate.

Ricki shrugged. "He looked hungry."

"I thought," said Vanessa, smiling, "you didn't like him."

"Well . . ." Ricki gave another shrug. "Everybody gets cake at a birthday party."

In between licking strawberry frosting off his muzzle, Kirby panted at Ricki gratefully.

Vanessa gave him a pat on the head.

Suddenly he lunged upward and thanked Ricki with a huge, sugary kiss on the nose.

"Eeuu! Yuck!" Ricki yelped.

Wearing a broad doggie grin, Kirby cocked his head at her.

Vanessa doubled over laughing.

Ricki sighed and finally grinned back at Kirby. The trick to having a dog, and maybe to having a sister, too, probably had to do with knowing what to complain about and what to put up with.

"I know he loves me, but does he have to show it that way?" she asked Vanessa.

"You know what, Ricki?" her sister answered, still laughing. "I'm beginning to think that's exactly what families are for."

Fifth-grade fun from

BEATRICE GORMLEY

MORE FIFTH GRADE MAGIC 70883-3/$3.50/$4.25
When Amy uses her magic calendar to make her
wishes come true, things get out of control.

THE MAGIC MEAN MACHINE 75519-X/$2.95/$3.50
Alison Harrity can't beat Spencer at chess until
scientific genius Marvin helps her.

FIFTH-GRADE MAGIC 67439-1/$2.95/$3.50
Fifth-grader Gretchen Nichols would do anything to
have the lead in the school play—even believe in
magic!

And don't miss

MAIL-ORDER WINGS 67421-1/$2.95/$3.50
RICHARD AND THE VRATCH 75207-7/$2.95/$3.50
THE GHASTLY GLASSES 70262-2/$2.95/$3.50
BEST FRIEND INSURANCE 69854-4/$2.50/$2.95
PAUL'S VOLCANO 70562-1/$2.50/$3.25

MEET THE GIRLS FROM CABIN SIX IN

CAMP SUNNYSIDE FRIENDS

(#13) BIG SISTER BLUES	76551-9	($2.95 US/$3.50 Can)
(#12) THE TENNIS TRAP	76184-X	($2.95 US/$3.50 Can)
(#11) THE PROBLEM WITH PARENTS		
	76183-1	($2.95 US/$3.50 Can)
(#10) ERIN AND THE MOVIE STAR	76181-5	($2.95 US/$3.50 Can)
(#9) THE NEW-AND-IMPROVED SARAH		
	76180-7	($2.95 US/$3.50 Can)
(#8) TOO MANY COUNSELORS	75913-6	($2.95 US/$3.50 Can)
(#7) A WITCH IN CABIN SIX	75912-8	($2.95 US/$3.50 Can)
(#6) KATIE STEALS THE SHOW	75910-1	($2.95 US/$3.50 Can)
(#5) LOOKING FOR TROUBLE	75909-8	($2.95 US/$3.50 Can)
(#4) NEW GIRL IN CABIN SIX	75703-6	($2.95 US/$3.50 Can)
(#3) COLOR WAR!	75702-8	($2.50 US/$2.95 Can)
(#2) CABIN SIX PLAYS CUPID	75701-X	($2.50 US/$2.95 Can)
(#1) NO BOYS ALLOWED!	75700-1	($2.50 US/$2.95 Can)
MY CAMP MEMORY BOOK	76081-9	($5.95 US/$7.95 Can)

CAMP SUNNYSIDE FRIENDS SPECIAL:
CHRISTMAS REUNION　　76270-6 ($2.95 US/$3.50 Can)

Celebrating 40 Years of Cleary Kids!

CAMELOT presents
CLEARY FAVORITES!

☐ **HENRY HUGGINS**
70912-0 ($3.50 US/$4.25 Can)

☐ **HENRY AND BEEZUS**
70914-7 ($3.50 US/$4.25 Can)

☐ **HENRY AND THE CLUBHOUSE**
70915-5 ($3.50 US/$4.25 Can)

☐ **ELLEN TEBBITS**
70913-9 ($3.50 US/$4.25 Can)

☐ **HENRY AND RIBSY**
70917-1 ($3.50 US/$4.25 Can)

☐ **BEEZUS AND RAMONA**
70918-X ($3.50 US/$4.25 Can)

☐ **RAMONA AND HER FATHER**
70916-3 ($3.50 US/$4.25 Can)

☐ **MITCH AND AMY**
70925-2 ($3.50 US/$4.25 Can)

☐ **RUNAWAY RALPH**
70953-8 ($3.50 US/$4.25 Can)

☐ **HENRY AND THE PAPER ROUTE**
70921-X ($3.50 US/$4.25 Can)

☐ **RAMONA AND HER MOTHER**
70952-X ($3.50 US/$4.25 Can)

☐ **OTIS SPOFFORD**
70919-8 ($3.50 US/$4.25 Can)

☐ **THE MOUSE AND THE MOTORCYCLE**
70924-4 ($3.50 US/$4.25 Can)

☐ **SOCKS**
70926-0 ($3.50 US/$4.25 Can)

☐ **EMILY'S RUNAWAY IMAGINATION**
70923-6 ($3.50 US/$4.25 Can)

☐ **MUGGIE MAGGIE**
71087-0 ($3.50 US/$4.25 Can)